Pandora's Box

by

Jack Walsh

Front Cover Image

Pandora (1882)

by

Jules Joseph Lefebvre (1836 – 1911)

Pandora's Box
is dedicated to

Unrequited Love

Table of Contents

I will rise now, and go about the city in the streets, and in the broad ways, I will seek him whom my soul loveth: I sought him, but I found him not.

The watchmen that go about the city found me: to whom I said, Saw ye him whom my soul loveth?

Song of Solomon, Chapter 3, Verses 2 and 3.

King James Bible.

Statement of Glen McKinley: Spring 2017

I have been in some very dark places in recent times and as I write, I am in a darker place than I have ever been. It is so dark (within my mind, you understand) I do not believe I will ever see the mental light of day again. I am travelling along that dark, dark tunnel we have all experienced at one time or another (well, none of us are perfect) and I can say with many degrees of absolute certainty that there is no light at the end of this one. At the very least, not for me there isn't.

****

Can witches, in this modern day and age, cast spells? Can ghosts physically harm you? Do evil spirits truly exist or are they, as Dietrich Weissman very firmly believes, a mere figment of our imagination; something we invent when we are, like me, sick in the head? Are they a sign of a truly screwed up psyche? And do the dead come back to haunt us, to seek retribution, to settle scores? If they do, then I hope and pray I'm not around when they come calling.

Children can be vicious without reason. So can their mothers. It is that natural motherly protection they drape around their children. My wife is still alive and has threatened horrendous things if she ever gets her hands on me. But my children are dead. I stabbed and slashed and cut and sliced and hacked them to death: Amelia, aged ten years, Joseph, aged twelve years and Charlie (short for Charlene) aged six years, may come knocking on my cell door one day seeking to gain entry and ultimate revenge for what I did to them.

The prospect of this happening frightens me beyond imagination. It does indeed because for some years now, five years, I think, I have been hearing scratching noises at my cell door and I only hear it in the early hours of the morning when all is quiet and all of the insane people have finally fallen into a sort of sleep (the sedative drugs taking a hold, you understand). Sometimes, it happens every night and to the point where it drives me stir crazy, yet at other times, it is only every few nights and then sometimes, it stops altogether. I get to thinking it is just my imagination and it won't come back, perhaps a weird side effect of the medication I'm taking. But then it begins again and always returns with a sense of ferociousness, as if whoever is doing it is catching up on lost time and is desperate to gain entry.

Sometimes, it is very loud and I can hear children laughing as the noise continues and the laughing is evil beyond belief; yet, at other times, the scratching sounds are barely noticeable. Can you hear it? You will if you listen very carefully.

I once told Professor Weissman about this but he just gave me a sympathetic look, smiled and said something like, "We'll increase your medication so you can get a good night's sleep."

How stupid is that? Is medication going to prevent my dead kids scratching their way into my cell in order to do horrendous things to me? Will medication prevent them from breaking through the steel door and torturing me to death?

Professor Weissman, if I promise to be good, really, really good, if I offer you my most excellent promise of impeccably good behaviour, will you stop my children scratching their way through my cell door to do whatever it is they intend to do to me? I know it's three inches of solid steel but children can be very resilient, especially when they are seeking revenge and have murder in mind and they have an eternity to do whatever they have planned to do. Thus, time is on their side.

If you do this for me, I promise to be really very, very good. But I'll tell you something – and this has to remain a secret betwixt me and thee. There is a tiny gap, oh, about one quarter of an inch, between the floor and the bottom edge of the door. Don't let on to my kids about this because I don't think they have discovered it yet and I don't want them to. I fear they could quite easily slip through that gap. Maybe that is how Susie and Donna get in (more about Donna later). Or do they get in via my head? I don't know. All I know is I keep worrying about my kids getting in.

But of course! *That* is how Susie and Donna get in; they simply float *through* the door because they enjoy an ethereal existence in the spirit world. And maybe they do get through that tiny space between the floor and the bottom of the door. It isn't important. They get in, is all.

My kids could get in that way too but, regardless of how many years it takes, they simply want to scratch their way through the three inches of solid steel just to torment me. They know that I know they can have me any time they like but the little bastards simply want to torment me for however long it takes. And they can wait for an eternity because they know eventually I will die and they know where I will be going to. And where I'm going to, I won't be hearing heavenly angels playing on their harps! More like a weeping and gnashing of teeth. Their teeth and my weeping!

****

Well, good people, maybe you want to listen to my story. Or have you simply come to gloat, as if I'm an excitable macaque monkey in a steel cage in Central Park Zoo and here I am merely for your entertainment? Would you like a banana, macaque? What about some peanuts? Monkeys eat bananas and peanuts, don't they? Er...no, not really. It's just like saying elephants eat buns. Animals eat what they can get, you bunch of schmucks!

No, I'm not a monkey. I'm human – contrary to my ex-wife's opinion. She thinks I'm an unmitigated monster and mayhap she is right on that score – but I still have no recollection of what I did – correction, what I am *supposed* to have done.

I don't know many of the answers to all of Professor Weissman's questions. He keeps asking me the same questions over and over – they sound different each time, but they are basically the same questions. I was thinking perhaps you could, after reading this account of things, guide me with your own opinions. As Hannibal Lecter would say: Thrill me with your acumen.

You can either listen to me or my illustrious team of psychiatrists, led by Dietrich Weissman, who was recently made an Emeritus Professor of Forensic Psychiatry no less. But regardless of his qualifications, it doesn't necessarily mean he knows everything there is to know about my case. He and his team will tell you a very different story to mine but that is their business and none of my own. They are governed by rules and convention and facts which they can see and not what they cannot see and know.

I am told I will spend the remainder of my rotten life here so I really do not have any reason to lie to you. What will I gain if I lie to you? What I say happened did happen and why the psychiatric team's opinion is different is totally and utterly beyond my understanding.

I know Susie came back from the dead; of that I am utterly certain. It was she who made me slash and hack my children to ribbons. The psychiatrists think otherwise. They think it was me and me alone and who am I to argue with such collective knowledge? But however they think, collectively or individually, doesn't concern me. It was Susie's guiding hand - you know what I mean. Susie made me kill my dog – I know she did and although no fingerprints were found on the knife (mine or hers) she was entirely responsible. Or to put it another way, she *made me* do it.

Susie was (is) a very insanely jealous woman and she didn't want me to have anyone or anything in my life but her. Not the kids, not the dog, not even the fucking goldfish for Christ's sake!

So it matters not what the psychiatrists think. It is of no great importance to me because so long as I know the truth, nothing, absolutely nothing else matters.

So let me tell you all about it. Why not? I have nothing else to do except sit and stare at these four padded walls and the padded floor. And when I learn to walk on the ceiling, they may add padding to that as well.

I have a lifetime in which to tell my story. Perhaps because it is due to the fact they have classed me as being clinically insane and until the New York State Court says otherwise (under Dietrich Weissman's expert guidance), here I will remain.

If they ever send me to an ordinary prison, the guys in there will tear me to pieces. You know what they do to kiddie killers, don't you? But best leave that to your own imagination.

But no, there is no way the Supreme Court will ever let me out of here. Why should they when I laughed (low but audibly) throughout my sentencing hearing? My attorney resigned from the New York State legal system after the case and took himself off to the wilds of Canada. That's okay, buddy. I understand how it is with you. I have no plans to come calling.

He was practically crapping himself at the hearing because he suddenly came to realise I really was well and truly insane. I don't think he had met an insane person before and I must have frightened him very badly.

****

And now here I am, very securely locked away. As I said in

my brief history of Mockingbird Heights (you can read it later in this text), I have read and interpreted the family diaries thoroughly. To simply reprint them here would be a tedious task and they would make an even more tedious read. So this is my own faithful interpretation of events.

And thus, here is a tale to be twice told.

Manhattan – Staten Island: 2005 - 2008

And this is where I first come in. I walked into this whole goddamn affair like a schnook. I had my eyes closed and let it wash all over me. This is where the script isn't conjecture or stuff I think might have happened or might have been said. This stuff isn't in the various family diaries. This, Dietrich Weissman, my psychiatrist friend, is the real stuff that happened. I know it happened because I was there at the time. I experienced it and sometimes, it scared the living shit out of me, so if you are in any doubt as to its authenticity, well, I suggest you fill out a TS form (Tough Shit to you, Professor) because for professional reasons, your version of the truth has to be different to mine. I don't care. I have greater things to worry about. However, what you will get later is the history of the decline of this family and all of the dirt and putrefaction and goddamn rottenness that brought it to such an ignominious end. But has it ended? Judge for yourself, sport. Mine will always be the last word.

****

Everybody gets what he wants and for my sins, I got Susie. I committed a lot of sins with Susie because she wanted me; she wanted me to travel all the way along this strange highway with her. Susie was insatiable with regard to her voracious sex life and her desire to reach the heights and depths of her wanton depravity was as limitless as any human emotion could be and I was more than a willing passenger, very willing to go all the way with her.

For those first few months, she was totally and utterly desirable and irresistible and who could possibly turn his back on her and say, "No thanks, honey." She was like a siren, attracting all who got too close inside her field of magnetism – over which she had total and complete control.

Susie, the fire and passion of my soul and ultimately,

my nemesis. Susie, the queen bitch of the universe.

****

She engineered the way we got together, although she always maintained it was by pure chance. No, it was not! Women like Susie make plans to the extent that they never go wrong and Susie planned this one down to the very last infinitesimal micron of detail. She planned it with the knowledge that because she knew men and their weaknesses and their most secret desires, she wanted me, she was going to have me and nothing and no one was going to stop her from getting what she wanted.

I remember only too well that first night our eyes met. It was just a quick glance but it set me further along a path I should never have trodden in the first place (but I will relate my adventure with Livia soon enough).

I was with a few friends at a Japanese restaurant in Greenwich Village and we were eating sushi and getting involved with another woman after my marriage to Anna had ended in a very expensive and acrimonious quickie divorce was the very last thing on my mind. I was enjoying my freedom, although I was very much saddened by the collapse of my marriage and I still had an urge, a determination rather, to go some way to healing the rift between Anna and myself, but at that particular moment in my life, I had no intention of there being another Mrs. Glen McKinley.

I had had a few affairs since the divorce but they never lasted long; they always fizzled out after a few weeks. My heart simply was not in it. But even so, I had respect for them, even though the affairs were so brief. Hey, come on! What's wrong with a little respect? Okay, so I slept with one or two of them; it's the human condition, the nature of man to relieve himself of the pressures and stresses of the day and who better to relieve that stress than an attractive woman? I never saw any of them as a cheap one night stand. I was far more refined and respectful than that.

Our eyes had met more than a few times during the evening and it seemed every time I glanced in her direction, she was giving me the eye; but she never smiled and her piercing eyes were not smiling either and I found that to be…ah…a little creepy? It was like she was looking inside of me, down to the depths of my soul to see what it was that made me tick.

So when she got up from her table (I honestly thought she was going to come across to my table and ask who I thought I was staring at?) and walked towards the door to leave, she passed by me and dropped her pocketbook. It landed virtually at my feet. I bent down to pick it up and called after her as she was half way through the door – "Excuse me, Miss, you've dropped your…" – but she was gone, like the puff of a light summer breeze. She was gone, but her perfume and image remained like an afterglow.

When my friends left, I looked inside the pocketbook (a Louis Vuitton). There was a platinum American Express card, a Christian Dior lipstick, a small bottle of Chanel No. 5 (she obviously had very expensive tastes), five hundred dollars in tens and twenties and a business card with her name, business address (J. P. Morgan Chase), telephone number (business) and her photograph in colour. Her light olive skin and her name gave a clue to her Spanish ancestry of which she was (I later discovered) the third generation of the joining of the Saul and de Francia families.

There were also a few sundry items: half a dozen keys on an 18 carat gold keyring (I tend to notice the small details), an address book (expensive looking and leather bound), a pack of Cohiba Mini Cigarillos and an 18 carat gold Dunhill cigarette (cigarillo?) lighter. Yes, she most definitely had very expensive tastes. I liked her already. Simply liked her and nothing more.

On the reverse of the business card was what appeared to be a private telephone number. The business card told me she headed a foreign currency dealership within J. P. Morgan Chase and thus, I had as much information on Miss Susie de Francia as I needed in order to return the property.

I know I should have handed the pocketbook in to the restaurant management and left them to deal with it, but I did no such thing. Something made me hang on to it. I was curious about her. I wanted to get to know her. She interested me. More than that, she intrigued me and what we then did over the next three years, well, there is no going back. Not now. Not ever.

****

It was one of those occurrences when you wish you could go back in time and instead of taking the path you actually did take, you fervently wish you had taken another. But the choice is yours and it's always a fifty fifty gamble. But the cause of my woes was not Susie (at first). She came later. It was Livia (soon, so have patience) who helped me to begin my irreversible slide into eternal night.

I called her at her office and when I managed to get past her secretary, I was surprised at the softness, the gentility of her voice and manner.

"You dropped your pocketbook in Miyabi Sushi Restaurant," was my opening gambit. "I was there last evening and it slipped away from you as you walked by my table."

"Were you the gentleman in the navy blue sport jacket with brass buttons?"

"The very same."

"I thought so. Did you look inside at the contents?"

"Yes. I needed a contact number for you. I should have left it with the restaurant manager but something told me to take charge of it myself."

"And you found the contact number."

"Yes, I found it. Miss de Francia, I must say you have some rather expensive tastes. I know some women who might even kill for the contents of your pocketbook."

"It comes with the job. I can't be expected to turn up at the office in torn jeans, scuffed sneakers and carrying a tote bag. Those are my comfy clothes at home for the weekend and most definitely not to be seen at 270 Park Avenue."

"Yes, I know J. P. Morgan Chase quite well. I'll deliver it to your office this lunchtime."

"Why don't we meet at a restaurant? There's a cosy little Sicilian…"

"Are you hitting on me, Miss de Francia?"

"Maybe, but just at the moment inviting you out to lunch. Look upon it as a reward for keeping the lost property on my behalf."

So I collected her from her office at 270 Park Avenue and we took lunch together – but at her expense. She insisted with a passion and I was not prepared to argue the point.

We ate at a Sicilian restaurant on West Forty Fifth and the restaurant served a superbly rich and very potent red wine. She knew how to wine and dine a guy and performed the function with such finesse, it was almost as if she had a very specific talent for entertaining.

But who was Susie? What was she made of? How did she function in the very masculine world of banking and currency dealing?

At first sight, she could have been any prim and proper young lady in her late twenties or early thirties, (she was thirty-three) but she hid much and it only came to the surface when it was tempted to do so or when she so desired it. But we can never understand any person unless we truly know them and to know them, you have to reach down into the depths of the heart and soul to even begin to find any answers. It takes months in a new relationship, even years, and even into the realms of marriage (maybe even a divorce?).

Some aspects of a person we later find to be most pleasant and rewarding, perhaps pleasantly surprising, perhaps something hidden just below the surface until it is time to show its face: it makes us smile, knowing we have made the right choice.

But it is the dark side of the human psyche, that which lies deeply buried, which tends to catch our attention, makes us curious to want to know more – if we manage to catch a glimpse of it. But more often than not, we do only catch rare glimpses of it and such rare glimpses may either encourage us to explore further, even though we may realise, if we are intelligent enough, the journey may be fraught with danger, or leave well alone. Fortunately, such aspects of the dark side of human nature remain well hidden for the most part until a catalyst induces a metamorphosis to help bring it to the surface.

Susie kept her dark side to herself (for a while) and there was only the merest hint of a glimpse through the protective shield she threw around herself. She was as beautiful as beautiful can ever be and as yet, I could see no flaw which might tell me this might be our one and only date. She was not what you might call stunningly attractive (strangely, that would have spoiled her looks) but I have always had the opinion that if you can describe someone as being stunningly attractive, then the woman in question is flawed in some way. Pick a dozen or so Hollywood starlets, read the press reports and the Hollywood gossip columns and you will begin to understand my meaning. There are only three types of people that populate Hollywood; stars, dentists and plastic surgeons.

Yes, Susie was beautiful; not your average caked in makeup Barbie Doll type of false beauty, but a real natural. There was nothing, absolutely nothing, false about her physically stunning beauty, which combined a strong magnetic attraction. Her dark and slightly curly brunette hair added to the attraction, along with her perfectly formed thin lips (she wasn't your average pouty kind of beauty). But her eyes: I was wary of her starkly coloured green eyes. I felt as if they hid something she didn't want me to see. Perhaps it was just me, my imagination playing games. But those eyes were most definitely not the windows to her soul because I could see nothing through or behind them and when I finally discovered the soul within her, I firmly understood why she never allowed anyone but a close relationship entry to her very private world.

She had poise. She had flair. Yet it seemed men might be afraid to approach her. Not because of fear of the embarrassment of rejection, but perhaps they sensed something such as I had done briefly when we first set eyes on each other in the Myabi Sushi Restaurant.

And me? What was it about me that she could possibly like? Now don't get me wrong; I'm not doing myself down but I've not long been through an horrendous divorce (because Anna found me in bed with the *au pair*. She was fired and I was kicked out of the house). There is something inside of me which tells me I must make a serious attempt at screwing every attractive woman under the age of twenty-five but for the most part, I always managed to resist. Not with Livia though. She was a temptress and I paid a heavy price for my dalliance with her. In fact, the price was far too heavy.

It happened on an afternoon when Anna said she was working late because she had a meeting at the hospital at four in the afternoon and such meeting was likely to continue into the late evening.

Take some advice, my friend, from someone who knows; never, ever trust for the important people invited to a meeting to actually turn up at the meeting. It was a budgets meeting and Richard Stein, the Head of Finance, was sunning himself in Grand Bahama, and Misters Riker and Schonbrunner (Principal of the Medical School and Chief Specialist Surgeon) were not available because of other more important commitments. Thus, the meeting was cancelled and Anna arrived home very much earlier than expected.

The first I realised something was wrong was when Livia changed her point of vision from my eyes (she was on top of me and facing the door to the bedroom) to beyond me where Anna was standing at the bedroom door pointing a loaded shotgun in our direction. And then there was that little giveaway gasp from Livia's lips and a, "Get off my husband, you conniving little slut," from Anna which wiped the smile off her face. I knew the shotgun was loaded because I removed the live cartridges when I managed to coax the gun from Anna. We used to use it for skeet shooting and I didn't want her using it on me – or Livia – especially when she gently poked my nuts with the end of the barrel.

Oh boy but was I simply scared or scared shitless?

"Be very careful with that, Anna. It only needs about three pounds of pressure to release the hammers and it looks like you're just an ounce or two shy of the mark. That buckshot can do a lot of damage."

"I know exactly what damage it can do. I've seen what a barrel-load of buckshot can do to a clay pigeon, so your soft flesh won't be a problem. Oh look! It's *all* gone soft all of a sudden! Find yourself a new boyfriend, Livia. He obviously can't keep it up all that long. And certainly not in a crisis."

"Anna, it doesn't mean anything," I said and it sounded like one of my famous clichés.

"You bastard," Livia yelled as she swiped my face with the palm of her hand. "You said you loved me!"

"Oh for Christ almighty's sake!" Anna yelled and I swear she put another couple of ounces of pressure on the trigger. "Can't you think of something better than that? It's an ages old cliché, darling, which doesn't do it for me. The both of you! Well for heaven's sake will one of you answer?"

"No. I don't know...I..."

"No? You don't know? What is it you do know, Glen? Absolutely nothing because you have your testosterone-filled brains hanging either side of your dick? Let me make it easy for you. I'll tell you what I know. Our daughter of twelve months is sleeping in her cot a few doors away and instead of doing her job – which I pay her over the odds to do – I find the domestic help is butt naked in *my* bed and fucking my husband!"

"Anna, this isn't what it seems."

"Typical lothario – full of clichés and full of shit. Don't you know anything but clichés? Don't bother answering that. Okay, here is what we are all going to do. Livia, you can get dressed, get your stuff packed and get the hell back to sunny Geneva from whence you came and you can pay for your own flight ticket or train ticket or cab fare to the next employer's bed or wherever you are going. And don't bother asking for a reference.

"Glen, I'm not going to be so openly harsh on you but you have three days in which to find an apartment – I don't think you will find anything within five miles of here. Correction – I don't *want* you to find anything within five miles of here. Tell you what, Glen, stay in the city. When you have found an apartment, move into it with everything you own. I'm filing for divorce and the children remain with me. But until you hear from me, do not come anywhere near this home and do not approach Amelia or Joseph at their school."

"I wasn't going to."

"You would if you could." She turned to Livia, who was still kneeling on the bed and covering herself with the sheets. "Are you still here? I thought I told you to leave my home. Do so within the next fifteen minutes or I will personally throw you out on to the street as you are and like the trash you are."

I don't know why, but I timed her. It was within a second or two, literally, of fifteen minutes. From the time she started dressing, then packing, then closing (slamming) the door at the front of the house - just a smidgen shy of fifteen minutes. Anna looked disappointed that she couldn't manhandle her out of the house.

****

So here I was with Susie in a Sicilian restaurant eating Caponata (made to an old Sicilian recipe which included lobster and swordfish, tuna roe and shrimp) followed by Cannoli Piana Degli Albanese. I casually reminded Susie that white wine should be taken with the Caponata but she replied quite casually (and mayhap this might have been a hidden warning shot), "I usually get what I want, Glen, and I want red wine. You can have white if you want it."

"No, no. red is fine. This has a kick like a mule. Hey, there I go with my clichés again."

****

I should have tried to look deeper inside her from the very beginning and maybe then I might have found the moral strength to try and patch things up with Anna. I don't blame her for her words and actions on the day she threw Livia out of the house and then gave me a three day ultimatum, but Anna was very quick to calm down and now I wish I had bided my time. To quote another Glen McKinley cliché: Everything comes to he who waits. Not exactly a proper cliché – and it does sound rather selfish – but you know what I mean.

But now there was Susie. I fell willingly into her spider's web and doing the kind of things we did over our time together, particularly during the first few months, is akin to what you might find in trashy pornographic fiction some of the lower class book outlets seem to stock – but *never* in places like Barnes and Noble in New York or Foyles in London! But you have this idea it can never really happen in real life. It can only happen in some weirdo's insane fantasy.

Yes, I should have looked deeper inside instead of thinking: ah, what the hell.

Inside, she was rotten and ugly to the core. She fully knew of her desires and the seemingly impossible uncharted depths of her depravity and her depravity was insane. Susie was insane. What drove her to do these things, perform these acts and goading me into helping her, was insane. She had to be completely twisted if she gained any degree of pleasure from the things she did to me and what she asked me to do to her. But she most definitely did gain a lot of pleasure from it.

She would say anything to me when she wanted to indulge her fantasies and she was never coy about asking: you know, when you want your wife or girlfriend to do something out of the ordinary to you or she wants you to do something to her but you are both afraid to ask in case it brings forth a rejection and mayhap a snort or two of disgust or derision that you would even consider sinking so low and be so depraved as to wanting to get your sexual kicks in such a manner.

But she was flawed, very seriously flawed and it seemed I discovered the flaw after I had become well and truly stuck on the gossamer strands of her spider's web. What a tarantula she was! What a...what a monstress!

She broached the subject not many weeks after the first time we made love at her home on Staten Island. It was superb the first time and every time after that – when it was normal and straightforward sex. But after a month or six weeks of normality, she said something quite bluntly and which knocked me back a ways.

I knew from the very first lovemaking session she liked to hike things up a smidgen – but a smidgen was enough for me and what she did that first time was slightly more than a smidgen. It was good, it was exciting and it brought something unusual to the proceedings.

When we emerged from the same Sicilian restaurant (it had become a regular haunt for us) on one of our dates, I told her the red wine was winning its battle and I was going back to my apartment to sleep it off. She said she had a far better idea and we took a cab to the Manhattan Ferry Point at the Whitehall Terminal. Then we took the ferry to the St. George Terminal on Staten Island where she had her car parked.

I was impressed with the car. It was a Series Three E-Type Jaguar and very carefully painted in British Racing Green. I later discovered she had rescued it from the barn of a farm in Vermont she happened to be driving passed and they were having a yard sale. She bought the car (which wasn't actually in the sale) for a couple of thousand dollars (apparently, it was in a god-awful state) and spent a small fortune on having it restored. It was now a very carefully looked after piece of engineering, a classic auto in every sense.

I was also impressed with her single storey home on Fayann Lane in the Tottenville District of Staten Island and my eighteen mile ride from the ferry terminal to her home was an experience any sports car aficionado would kill for, especially when accompanied by a beautiful woman.

But I guess I had had it for the day. That Sicilian red wine packed a punch as powerful as any Jack Dempsey could throw and I collapsed on a bed in one of the three bedrooms and slept like I hadn't slept for days.

****

I thought that would be the end of it. I wasn't exactly drunk but I doubt I would have passed the test if the police had pulled me over on the highway. She would drive me to the ferry terminal the next morning, we would say: So long, I'll call you tomorrow – and we would go our separate ways.

But I woke at eight in the evening and Susie was standing at the side of the bed. All she had on was a transparent peignoir, a brassiere and panty set, with matching garter belt and nylons – all in black and I remember thinking: This must be a dream. This has to be a dream.

But it was no such thing because I suddenly became aware that I was butt naked (I remember falling asleep fully clothed) and I only had a hand towel covering a rapidly approaching hardening of a certain part of my physique – and the towel was becoming grossly misshapen.

"Glen," she said. "Welcome back to reality. I have a question to ask you. Do you know what making love is about?"

"I…I think so. I mean…er…making kids? Thinking

how jealous the other guys are because they aren't riding shotgun? This question has completely thrown me. Is there a point to this and did you undress me?"

"Well, you didn't do it yourself. I'll tell you what it's about. It's about being able to please your partner in an exquisite way, something they will look forward to the next time and all the times after that– or maybe it will be something a little different. When you consider doing something unusual to your partner, keep it to yourself and it will invariably turn out to be a most pleasant surprise. Never give away any clues. You think I'm giving away a clue now?"

"That's the way it looks to me."

"Wrong. There is an adjunct to this, only in my opinion, and because I desire it, it is an essential adjunct. To make this work, I have to be a good actress. And I'm a good dancer too. I went to dance school for a few years when I was fifteen and sixteen. They called me a natural but there is very little money in being a dance professional so when I was eighteen, I went to Columbia Business School and studied banking, finance and economics. I graduated valedictorian with an MBA and went straight into dealing currency. Do you like music, Glen?"

"Well…yes. What's your taste in music? I hope we don't clash on the subject."

"Something with a beat, a definite beat – soft or hard. And something – excitingly sensual. But don't worry. We won't clash on the subject of music. I'm rather hoping the music and dance will help to raise that growing bulge beneath the towel just a smidge more so we can have long term stiffness.

"Do you have a dark side, Glen?"

"I can't say that I have one."

"Yes, you do have a dark side. Everybody has a dark side. You don't realise you have it because you haven't explored it as much as you should. Or you have totally ignored it. Perhaps at one point you have been frightened of it. You shouldn't do that. You should always explore your deepest desires. And it depends at what depth inside of you it exists. But somehow, I don't think it will be difficult for me to reach inside and touch your darkness. Cue the music."

And she pointed a remote control to the tape deck in a corner of the bedroom.

She had the volume turned up and thus it was possible for me to clearly hear the opening bars of Ravel's *Bolero*. I then recalled a passage from Allan Bloom's *The Closing of the American Mind* (one of Anna's collection of text books, some of which I read occasionally) in which he says:

> *Young people know that rock has the beat of sexual intercourse. That is why Ravel's Bolero is the one piece of classical music that is commonly known and liked by them.*

He couldn't have been more right because Susie began to move in time with the rhythm of the music – and she knew how to move! She clasped her hands behind her head and sensually gyrated her hips; she lifted her ample breasts and tempted me by gently massaging my erection with them; she removed all items of clothing until she was naked. She gently swayed her breasts from side to side, then violently as the crescendo of the music increased and then gently again as she sank to her knees and dug her finger nails into my butt cheeks before she so very delicately touched me with her lips and the point of her tongue. Then she ate me a little more and then without warning (it had never happened before except perhaps the first couple of times I engaged in sexual shenanigans) I orgasmed and cried out loudly and with such force I thought: If this doesn't stop, I'll have a heart failure! And eventually, she fell back on to the bed and I entered her and when it finally happened for her, (it was far quicker than I expected) she howled and screamed and bucked like a bronco at a rodeo show until her orgasm was completely spent. She spent a long time regaining her breath. And this was no fake orgasm; it was real and I reckon I know fake from real. Good actress? She was Oscar quality and this was very real.

But it stopped. Eventually, it stopped and I sank slowly back to the bed and eventually I started breathing normally again.

"Oh my God, Susie. What did you do to me?"

"Well. I performed an erotic dance to erotic music and I think I may have given you the fellatio experience of a lifetime. It looks like I emptied your gonads of every last drop you had."

But she was always praising me, no matter how good she was.

"But you, Glen. Oh you are so good. You are…you are a master. You are an artisan. I must have you again along with Monsieur Ravel."

"I hate to say this, but I don't think I can go again tonight. Yes, you drained every last drop from me."

"That's okay. It's just a taste of things to come – two or three puns not intended."

****

It was a few months of regular dating and lovemaking before she broached the subject of her true desires. It was not that she was afraid to ask; she simply wanted to be certain of how I might take to a sudden and violent change in our bedroom habits.

Most of the time, she never thrusted and bucked like a wild horse on heat, simply reached out with her voice and tensed muscles to such impossible heights. I couldn't see it, if indeed it was a tangible thing to be seen. It sounded as if she was in extreme pain. I suppose yes she was, but there was a thousand fold amount of pleasure there too. She simply screamed her pain-pleasure, her orgasm, and reached for whatever was there.

And another time when she invited our mutual friend, Maurice Ravel, to a threesome. A minute from the end of the music, she shoved me back on the bed and straddled me (she liked to be in control) my very painful erection disappearing inside her and her violent in and out thrusting moved in time with the beat and crescendo of the music and howled like a banshee as she orgasmed out of control. I remember after the first time I had the pleasure of Monsieur Ravel, I went to a music store and purchased a compact disc of the piece – it was Leonard Bernstein and the New York Philharmonic and I think other music on the disc was George Gershwin's *Rhapsody in Blue* and some other orchestral pieces: I don't remember what they were.

"Where are we, Glen?," she said as she lay back on the bed and lit a cigarillo (I hoped to get her out of the habit of smoking in bed and had broached the subject a few times). "I mean in our relationship?"

"Well, in a good place I hope. Do you think we are in a good place?"

"Of course we are. But that isn't quite what I meant."

"Okay, so what did you mean?"

"I mean, how far do you dare to go? How far are you prepared to go to reach that nirvana of sexual ecstasy?"

"I thought I already had," I replied.

"No. I mean, can you go higher? Do you want to go

higher? Can you climb those impossible heights and meet me at the top? Because I've been there, Glen. I'm there now and I don't ever want to come down. Let me tell you part of my secret.

"When I come, when I orgasm, I go to heights you would not believe. I reach that peak of sexual ecstasy that other women would die for. But that secret is mine and mine alone."

"Not even for my ears?" I said.

"Yes, my lover, I'll tell you my secret. It is how I reach those heights, what I use to reach there."

"I'll tell you a story. I used to live with my great aunt and uncle. They adopted me when my mom passed on from this life. One day, my great aunt caught me reading a porno magazine, you know the type I mean – the ones you can only get from the back room of the sleazy stores which sell them. She was a very strictly religious person and she knew I knew what had happened to my mother – drink and drugs and the whole shebang, but you don't really want to know about that. She didn't want me to go the same way as her and so, sixteen as I was, she laid a thin bamboo cane across my ass a dozen or so times to try and teach me a lesson, but all she taught me was what I feel now. This was at a time not so many years ago when the way to punish your kids was not a darn good thrashing but a much more soft approach. Something more acceptable. But most definitely not Great Aunt Emilia. The soft approach was not her way.

"But hey, who cares? I learned a lot from the experience. And do you want to know something? I enjoyed it. Yes, I cried out but not for her to stop. It wasn't the pain. It was never the pain. No, after around the fourth or fifth stroke, I began to experience one orgasm after another and the ecstasy of it took me to heights I had never before achieved, even in my wildest girlish fantasies. She accidentally let me into a world I had not known before – and it only served for me to explore this dark world even more.

"I used to get the older guys from school to go into a store and get me the magazines. You know, get me a magazine and I'll let you feel my tits, sort of thing. And it worked."

I laughed heartily at this last statement. "Well, thank you very much, Doctor Kinsey, for the history lesson but I doubt if any of that was in the books he wrote. What an interesting life you have led. But I don't understand what it is you want and what it is I can give you."

She was not coy about what she wanted; she was as straightforward as anyone could be and it was like she was quoting terms of employment to me.

Basically, she was very much into sado-masochism; not heavily and not so much that it absolutely ruled every last part of her life (at least it didn't then). Don't get me wrong. She was not a Madame or Mistress or a professional dominatrix. She wasn't a hooker who hung around street corners waiting for passing trade. She didn't wear silly masks or dress herself up in all of that ridiculous leather and plastic and latex gear. No, that was never any part of the actress within her. She was more refined than that. What you saw was what you got – all woman and not a dressed up weirdo from Planet Bozo out for a quick spanking session.

This was very strictly private and confidential. She indulged in this strange behaviour to enhance her impossibly voracious sex life, as an interesting, if not unusual – and possibly dangerous - adjunct to it. It wasn't even a toy, something she could play with when she got bored. She was deadly serious about it and she warned me from the outset she would not be mocked.

And she had had a number of previous willing male partners (but only one relationship at a time – this was not the ancient Rome of Gaius Caligula: she warned me she was not into orgies) whom she cast aside when she tired of them or when their own sudden interest began to grow outside of her own set boundaries (or perhaps even when they became afraid of her true capabilities). But I guess they were much happier for the experience.

What she wanted from me was this (besides being a fully co-operative partner): she wanted me to hurt her. She wanted me to cane her. She wanted me to whip her. She wanted me to use electricity on her because she had an EEPS (Erotic Electrostimulation Power Source) violet wand in her basement (apart from a variety of whips and canes and an expensively made St. Andrew's Cross). And it always had to be here on Staten Island because the walls and ceiling of her basement were sound insulated. And when the mood would take her, she would want to do the same to me – and I guess that is why she never mentioned it as soon as our relationship started, in case I shied away and said: No thank you very much – and ride off into the sunset.

"It can't happen at your apartment because when either of us are on the receiving end, I don't want your neighbours interfering and calling the police."

And thus, throughout our relationship, I did whatever she demanded. But I will never forget the first time I became her 'willing' victim.

The following Friday, we lunched at the same Sicilian restaurant (but this time, I stuck to soda fizz – I didn't want to fall asleep at her home so hopelessly drunk I couldn't give a prize-winning performance).

We arrived at her home in the late afternoon. We ate a light salad snack, chit-chatted for a while and then showered (separately, on her insistence and me first – she had a thing about sex and cleanliness (it was one of her rules, I later discovered); I had no problem with that).

"Just keep the towel wrapped around you; don't get dressed," she said.

I showered, lay on the bed and smoked one of Susie's cigarillos (what a hypocrite: she had finally listened to me about not smoking in bed – and here was I doing the very same thing).

Susie emerged from the shower and when she shrugged off her towelling robe and placed a vicious looking three pronged leather tawse into my hand and said, "Use it on me, Glen. Make me earn my pain-pleasure and make me cry out for it," I thought: This is really for real!

"You're looking a little doubtful, Glen."

"I don't want to do this to you and then have you call the cops and have me arrested on an assault with battery charge."

"Don't be so naïve. I'm serious about this, Glen. I've never been more serious about anything in my entire life. I know what I want and I want to teach you about what I want but if you think this is a silly child's game of show me yours and I'll show you mine, I'm afraid you are very much mistaken."

"You can have any man you want, Susie. You simply have to beckon him with your index finger and he is yours, like an obedient little doggie."

"But I don't want any man. And I don't want a prissy little doggie. I want you and only you. If I can't have you, what is there for me? Let me tell you something, Glen, so you will understand me a little more. I am not a cheap dime hooker and neither am I a high class escort or call girl. What I do I do for my own personal pleasure – and my partner's - and there is no financial gain, although if you happen to know a good tax accountant, I'll pay you a small commission for introducing me.

"What I do is done in the extreme privacy of my own home. I don't hang around some street corner in South Bronx or some waterfront flophouse waiting for passing trade. I don't crawl sidewalks until some pathetic john comes along looking for a quick thrill and I don't leave my cell phone number in telephone booths or porn store windows.

"I chose you, Glen, because you are what I want. My long search is over and I have you. All you have to do is submit to my desires. Use this tawse on me, Glen, and make me cry out for mercy. Make me use that word. Let that be our safe word. Make me suffer for my pain-pleasure. And when it is your turn to receive, I will give you the experience of a lifetime. You will wonder, besides the whip or cane, what hit you.

"Remember the first time we made love? If you have the right attitude, we can take each other to the Nth power of sexual ecstasy."

She closed my fingers around the handle of the tawse.

But I drastically underestimated her deepest desire for this kind of ritual.

"How hard do you want it?"

"As hard as you can. No quarter is asked, none is to be given – but in carefully measured strokes."

At first, I was like a child learning its ABC because this was totally alien to me and I had never once broached the subject of strange sex to any of my previous female friends, including Anna. Strangely though, being a clinical psychiatrist and a damn good one, yes, perhaps she would have understood, though I wonder if she might have tried to analyse me and then talk me out of it; perhaps her way of saying no when she fully realised that two naked people in the bedroom sometimes engage in strange and exciting practices (by mutual agreement).

But understanding is not doing and simply playing around with a leather tawse like it was a cheap sex toy was most definitely not what Susie wanted.

She blew up in my face. "Oh for Christ almighty's fucking sake, Glen! Do you not know how to use a simple strip of leather on naked skin?"

"No...I've never..."

"Did your father never use his leather belt on you? My great aunt used leather on me more than a few times and my grandmother used it on my mother. And a bamboo cane too! It feels like you are using a goddamn feather across my butt and that is most definitely what I did not ask for. Goddamnit, do it like you mean it! Hurt me, Glen. Make me cry out for mercy and when I say that word, our very own safe word, know that I mean it and only then can you stop. And if I haven't orgasmed by then, well, I'm sure you can use your imagination on that score. Can you comply with that? Can you truly give me what I want? Can you truly go all the way with me, Glen McKinley? You have to go much further than you have ever gone in your wildest dreams."

"But...but..." I stammered.

"Oh for the love of Christ! I'll show you exactly what it is I want from you!"

She grabbed me by the upper left arm and practically frog-marched me toward her basement. But once through the door of the lounge she turned on me and swung her right fist and it connected with my jaw and she knocked me for six. I was aware of movement but I felt powerless to do anything. I felt completely under her control.

When I came back to reality, I was in the basement.

She had either carried me down or dragged me down; but it doesn't matter which. Something told me she had remarkable physical strength. She had at the very least managed to tie a loop of thick silk cord around each wrist and hoisted me so that one end of the loop on each wrist could be attached to a steel hook screwed into the timbers of the ceiling beams from which I was suspended – well, at least my feet touched the floor.

"Welcome back to reality, Glen," she said. "These items I hold in my hand? Let me explain what they are so there will be no mistake. These, by the way, are not toys or things to play around with when you are bored. They are used for a specific purpose – to cause pain, to subjugate a willing subject, to teach the subject in question the error of his or her ways.

"This is called a whip. As you can see, it has a single strand, thick at one end and thinning out at the other end. It requires a good deal of practice in order to use it correctly. When used upon the subject – excuse the obvious – it hurts and it can draw blood.

"This is also a whip but it is smaller and has seven strands of supple leather, each of them one quarter of an inch wide and one sixteenth of an inch in thickness. Each strand is twenty-four inches in length. It does not require so much accuracy as a longer single strand whip but when used on the subject, again, it hurts and it also can draw blood."

And then she opened a long draw which covered almost the length of a mahogany leather top desk.

"Here is a selection of canes, horsewhips, leather straps, what have you – all designed for a single purpose and when applied correctly, they also hurt and most of them can draw blood.

"This, as you know, is a tawse. It is made entirely of

supple leather and consists of a handle with three prongs of leather. It was originally designed for use in schools of long ago in Scotland and England and specifically for use on the hands, but I prefer to use it elsewhere – as you will soon discover. When used correctly, it does not draw blood but believe me, it hurts.

"There against the wall is the St. Andrews Cross or the *Crux Decussata*, and it takes its name from the type of cross that Saint Andrew was crucified on. It has modifications but as an instrument to subjugate while receiving punishment, it is perfect.

"So this is my very private den and you only enter this room for one reason and one reason only: to punish or be punished. Do you understand me, Glen?"

"Yes, I do. I fully understand."

"Good. So when I tell you to use one of these on me, I mean business. I don't mean for you to tickle my skin with whatever, like it's a silly little boy or girl sex game we play when our parents aren't looking. I intend you to beat me with them, lay them on my flesh so that I writhe in pain and scream for mercy. That is our code word to stop immediately. I always do but I have to trust you to do the same. Can you do that, Glen?"

"Yes, I think so."

"Yes, you think so? What I think is that you need to learn the rules, become a good actor and give me whatever my heart and soul desires."

She took the tawse in her right hand and moved behind me.

"Rule Number One."

And she swiped the tawse across my butt so hard, I yelped like a prince's whipping boy. Well, isn't that what I was supposed to be re-enacting? Or something like it?

"Rules are made to be obeyed. They are not intended to be broken or bent. If you obey the rules, discipline is maintained.

"Rule Number Two."

And she swiped me again with the tawse, even harder than the first time but I suspected she wasn't even trying all that hard. She was obviously well practised in this. I yelped again.

"Remember the safe word? Can you do that, Glen? Can you make me say that one word which is really such a simple word to spell but I want it to be difficult for both of us to say it. I have no problem with that because I have a very high pain barrier. Just remember when I told you my great aunt gave me a sound thrashing with a cane?

"And this is a cane. It comes in various thicknesses from thin and wispy to around one quarter of an inch, maybe even a third of an inch. I have all sorts and I also have several riding crops.

"Rules are not made to be interpreted. Thus, do nothing which will or is likely to endanger the relationship.

"Rule Number Three."

And she swiped me with the tawse again. It hurt, it stung, but something was happening, something was stirring from deep inside me and I liked what I was beginning to feel.

"There will be absolutely no penetration, especially when I am the subject. If there is and I do not consent to it, I will class it as rape and take it up with the police authorities.

"Rule Number Four."

She again struck me with the tawse and it stung worse than before, but this time, I was becoming very much aroused.

"Do not ever, even in the context of an ordinary relationship, but very specifically in the context of a master / mistress and subject scenario, use the language of the gutter. It is so unnecessary and I will not tolerate it. We use bad language when we are angry but when the subject is receiving punishment, there is no anger. There is only love and thus there is no need for angry words or words from the gutter.

"Rule Number Five."

She struck me again and I no longer cared about the hurt and the stinging and how the cheeks of my butt must be smarting. All I knew was I was getting the biggest and hardest erection I had ever experienced.

"When either of us uses the code word, that is the signal for everything to stop immediately – and I mean immediately! Not one second after, not one lash of the whip or one stroke of the cane afterward.

"Rule Number Six."

And I received stroke number six. My erection was becoming eager and painful but I guessed I had to hang on to the best of my ability. I had to find inner strength, perhaps the inner strength Susie expected me to have, to control what was happening inside of me. And neither did I want to disappoint Susie.

"When you fetch blood, that is the time to stop and think, to ask if the subject wishes to continue. This is where Rule Number Five also applies.

"Rule Number Seven."

And she gave me a seventh stroke of the tawse, but I had myself under control. I knew what her game was at this moment and I had presented her with the grandest of opportunities. Something told me I was pleasing her out of all expectations and this pupil would not take too long to learn.

"There are certain parts of the human body which are taboo when undergoing an experience. You already know that penetration will not take place unless you have my consent. I will also tell you that never – never! – will I permit anal penetration. I personally think it to be an abhorrent practice, sickeningly disgusting, and I will not even consider entertaining the idea.

"Rule number eight.

"There will be no use of whips, canes or other suchlike ephemera on the front of the body during an experience. Between the shoulder blades and to the base of the rib cage are acceptable providing there is no danger to damaging the spleen, liver or kidneys. The hindquarters and the top of the legs are the only areas you can use hand held instruments with any degree of safety but causing a maximum amount of pain

"Rule Number Nine."

The ninth stroke was harder than the rest and it made me wince and cry out. Now it was beginning to hurt. Now we were going into the realms of deep and very deep love and passion.

"Before any experience begins, you will shower or take a hot bath, void your insides, whatever. But there must be absolute cleanliness. If you think you can bend any of the other rules, this one is absolutely sacrosanct.

"Rule Number Ten."

I was not anticipating how much the tenth stroke would hurt. But it did hurt; not so much to make me cry out again but at that moment, I wished I had a leather sap to bite on. I thought I might suggest that to Susie. She might even agree to its use. But oh no, I had no intention of using the safe word for a long, long time.

"This will not be in any way, shape or form a dominatrix / submissive relationship but an integral part of a normal and loving relationship.

"And finally, Rule Number Eleven."

She laid the tawse across me again and I was falling into her clutches – and willingly! Oh how I was falling. My erection was so painful, I knew I would explode the very moment she touched me there. I so desperately wanted her to touch me but maybe she knew this and would make me wait.

"No other rules shall supersede these rules.

"Well, there you are, Glen. Those are my Eleven Commandments handed down to you from my very own lips. They are not to be disobeyed. If you want me, you can have me – but on my terms. And well done, Glen. Throughout that ordeal, you never once used the safe word and for that, you receive a very special reward."

Oh boy, but she had a very weird understanding of the word 'reward'.

She said, "You failed to give me what I wanted and now I want to show you exactly what I wanted and how it should have been administered."

And she went at me hell for leather (pun not intended) and after a while, she started yelling for me to say the safe word but I refused and held on. The pain was deeply hurtful but it was also erotically exciting.

But eventually, I said it, the safe word, and I hurt so much I was almost in tears and I couldn't sit properly for several days after unless I used a cushion or I was prepared to bear unbearable pain. I told the office it was a strained back muscle – and even then, I got a few smart-mouth comments from the guys who had seen me going out with a classy woman from J. P. Morgan Chase and there were a few strange looks from the women.

Somewhere along the line, Susie introduced a little game in that each of us would start out with one thousand dollars worth of casino chips and play poker until one party lost all of their money. The losing party had to submit to a flogging. I remember one time when I won the poker game (would you believe I had a hearts royal flush against her four nines – it isn't important but she was an expert poker player and she didn't lose all that often) and I flogged her but she refused to say the safe word – she flatly and vehemently refused to say it and she refused to follow even her own rules.

Eventually, though, I stopped when she finally screamed out our safe word. I went way over the top on that one – or rather she did - and it wasn't what I actually did that frightened me – she told me afterwards she thoroughly enjoyed the experience – but the deeply disturbing animal instincts that began to stir deep inside me. And here, I had opened up an entirely different world. To stem the tide of pain, she told me, she herself disappeared into another world where only the pain-pleasure of ecstasy reigned supreme and for most of the duration, she said she was totally lost in that world.

But I learned very quickly to give her what she and her rules demanded, every time she demanded it and throughout this morally destructive relationship, I became even bolder, to the extent that towards the end I was becoming very scared of what I might be truly capable. And that was not all, because I had to learn to be an actor in order to be able to give her the ultimate pleasure she so much desired. Simply to do it without adopting a second persona was far from good enough for Susie. Neither, if the truth be known, was it good enough for me. If it was simply me applying a whip or a cane to her naked derriere, it would have simply become a boring game before sex idea and we both would have soon tired of it. But it wasn't a game and the depths to which I myself was sinking were frighteningly deep and real.

When she came to her senses, when I had soothed her pain somewhat with a balm preparation, I said, "I should be angry with you, Susie, but I'm not."

"Why?"

"Because you didn't use the safe word until way beyond when I expected you to. You allowed me to carry on thrashing you and I could have hurt you more than I did."

"But I'm not angry with you," she replied.

"Why not," I said. "You have a right to be."

"No. I was testing my pain barrier to see what limit I could attain."

"But Susie, surely this is not a game of endurance like it is on some TV reality show. You can endure much pain because you are well experienced and because the endurance of pain is built into your genetic structure."

"I can handle it."

"No, you cannot. You can hardly walk as it is. Susie, let me add to your Eleven Commandments. If it looks as if it is going way beyond what we both class as normal, then whoever is administering must have the right to call a halt. Otherwise, things could go way beyond what they are supposed to. What if a serious injury occurs. Think about that, Susie. Think about it very carefully."

"I can't win, can I? "she said.

"Not this one," I told her. "We have to change the rules here for the good of both of us. I won't risk going beyond that barrier with you. I love you too much for that."

"And if you didn't love me?"

"Be serious, Susie. You know what I mean."

Yes, she knew what I meant but that did not alter the fact that I have seen her flog herself when I didn't have the courage to stop her because to have done so would have been to incur her wrath, her fury.

****

As time went on, we got deeper and deeper into the relationship and we truly loved each other. Susie was a smidge clingy but hey, who's perfect?

She said none of the rules could or should be broken. Well, none of them were but occasionally, they were bent to suit a particular direction. She forgave me for bending the rules and I reciprocated. But this was becoming a fairly frequent habit.

****

But there was one incident which sent our relationship into a steady but inevitable decline. It helped to develop a severe crack in our relationship and when I felt she was quite capable of taking this too far and killing me in a fit of uncontrollable rage. It happened, that's all. It was an unavoidable quirk of fate and when the incident was over, I was left thinking: How the hell am I going to finish this? Because it has to end. Because I cannot run the risk of this happening again. And it may well happen again. It is not mathematically impossible for it not to happen again – to any of the kids or to Anna herself.

She only used one of her instruments on me in truly uncontrolled anger one time and that was more than enough. I learned very quickly that Susie was not to be disappointed, let alone stood up.

I was nearly three hours late getting to her home and I could sense her fury simmering just below the surface of her being.

"You kept me waiting, Glen. Don't you dare ever keep me waiting. You are three hours late and there is no excuse for keeping me waiting."

"Susie, shush, shush now," and I put my arms around her to hug her but she shoved me away and yelled "No! Don't try this on me!"

"I'm really sorry for this, Susie, but my younger daughter was in the hospital with a fever. She's okay now but it could have been meningitis. I tried to call a number of times but your cell phone was switched off."

"I don't care! I don't give a damn! I should have been the centre of your attention!" And now she was screaming, screeching at the top of her voice and she was on the verge of losing control.

"Me! Me! Me! I should have been your one and only priority! I thought you were divorced! Couldn't you have got ex-wifey to do what was necessary?"

She didn't wait for an answer but she swiped me across the face with a massive right hook and the fact that she was wearing a knuckleduster most definitely contributed towards my state of unconsciousness.

When I finally came round (and with one doozy of a massive headache) Susie had dragged me down to the basement and secured my feet to one of the ceiling beams which left me hanging by my ankles. My wrists were handcuffed in front of me and a thin nylon rope ran round the handcuff chain and was secured to the rope binding my feet. I was completely naked and I remember saying to her (my voice trembled and I couldn't control it), "Susie, whatever you are thinking of doing, please don't. I can see you are angry and you may not be able to control yourself. We can talk about this."

"The time for talking, Glen, is over. I have allowed you to bend my rules – my rules! – and I own up to that error of judgement. It's my fault and mine only but you took advantage of it. You chose to break into a thousand pieces a most precious and unwritten rule to which you should have shown the highest possible respect. After this lesson, Glen, you will understand the meaning of the word 'respect' and you had better get it word perfect."

She was so angry when she said this. I knew she was in complete control but I also knew she was going to hurt me like she had never done before.

I knew she was strong but I never realised how strong she could be when she was angry. But her rage, on the surface at least, subsided into something she kept under complete control and over the next couple of hours, she used a series of thin bamboo canes on me in carefully and well spaced strokes with a mantra for each one.

The intensity of her retribution was such that she drove herself to tears, she was so desperate to reach down to the depths of her amoral corruption. Or perhaps her tears were for my suffering because although I used the safe word a considerable number of times, she ignored it every time.

I can't say if she laid on each stroke harder than the one before: perhaps not because each stroke hurt and made me jump (such as I could) and wince and I knew on several occasions I bit my lip (and my tongue once) severely cutting into the soft flesh of my lips and on a couple of occasions, I nearly choked as the blood ran up to the back of my nose.

And after each stroke, the mantra.

"You will never keep me waiting again."

"No others, except me, exist for you."

"You will never question my instructions again."

"If I tell you a certain time, I mean that very time, no sooner and certainly no later."

"You will do and use whatever I tell you to in order to bring me to the pinnacle of my desires."

"I exist for you to pleasure me and thus you will empty your thoughts of all others."

"Do not ask to be shown mercy in this time of my anger and retribution, because you do not deserve it."

"Clemency is a privilege which must be earned."

"It is not yours as a right."

"Do not expect to be given what you have not earned."

"If I tell you to submit to my deepest desires, you will do so without question."

"There is only me in your life and you will forsake all others for me."

…and on and on and on.

And when she tired of the bamboo canes (she broke two on me) she turned to electric shocks using the EEPS violet wand but I hurt so much from the canes, I was barely aware of it until she upped the voltage.

At that point, I must have passed out because when I came to, she was in tears and crooning over me, mopping my face with an ice cold cloth to help bring me round. But that vicious assault on me showed me a new side to her, one that told me she could be quite easily tipped over the edge by insane jealousy. It wasn't as if I screwed my ex-wife (I truly hadn't) but Susie didn't see it that way. As far as she was concerned, all of my attention should have been directed towards her and no one else for *whatever* reason.

I realised then what she was truly capable of and it need only be me innocently passing the time of day, perhaps only a few minutes with any woman and it might send her into a jealous rage. What if my car broke down on the way to her home and I couldn't call her because she had her cell phone switched off – again? What if I got involved in an auto accident? What if I fell ill? Susie was dangerous. Susie was teetering on the edge of dangerous insanity.

"You only felt some of what my mother used to get from my grandma for misbehaving. Let me tell you about it while you are recovering and while I'm massaging you with this curative balm. It will help take the soreness away and relax those knots in your muscles."

"Tell me another time, Susie. I can't concentrate right now."

"Don't try and be a hero. You are hurting and I have a duty to try and make things better for you. But we'll have our serious discussion another time if you want. I'll mark a date in my diary. But you have to know where I get my vicious streak from. And there is something and other things you really ought to know now.

"You can see the tainted seed in every generation of my family, right from my great grandfather's time and up to me. I still carry the tainted seed. It's in our genetic structure, but it dies with me, Glen. It dies with me because I am the last of my family. My great aunt and her husband passed on from this life ten years and twelve years ago respectively - they both had terminal cancers - so I really am the last of the line. Some years ago, I had a hysterectomy performed because I do not want children messing up my life. My life belongs to me and not to a bunch of wailing brats. I cannot have the seed regenerating or God alone knows what it will turn out to be like.

"My great grandfather raped my grandmother and

got her pregnant but she had the child aborted after a few months.

My grandmother murdered my grandfather by stabbing him to death because he raped my mother and grandma died in an asylum. Grandma went to the asylum because by the time the trial came around, she was really way off in doozyland.

My mother was a drug addict and alcoholic who was practically eaten alive by syphilis when the end came for her.

My great grandmother realised too late what a nasty little Pandora's box she had opened by refusing her husband any physical relationship after Athenia's birth and thus left him free reign to go womanising across the county. I think Athenia should have fought great grandpa off. I suspect she had the strength to fight him off. All of the females of our clan seem to be born with unnatural strength. It's in our genes. But at the same time, maybe she didn't believe it was happening, that it was all a horrible dream. I wonder if my great grandmother ever realised the significance of the name she was given at her birth.

"Do you remember that old Roger Corman movie *The Fall of the House of Usher* and how there was insanity and drunkenness and drug taking and incest in the entire family history? That movie could have been based on my family.

"But the tainted seed is sown and it enters each generation. I'm bad, Glen. I'm very bad."

And perhaps that is the only piece of true sanity I heard from her in the final months of our relationship. At least she was sane enough not to want to reproduce the rogue gene again.

"I keep diaries you know. It's a habit I inherited from my mother and grandmother. And great grandma too. They were prolific diarists. I have them all in boxes in the wine cellar. Instead of me telling you about my family, you can read the diaries and find out for yourself."

"I'll do that, Susie, but not right now. I want to go back to my own apartment but I can barely move."

"It'll take a few days, Glen. But again, you broke the rules and I couldn't let it pass."

"Leave it for now, Susie. Let's discuss it another time."

We left it at that and we never again got the opportunity to discuss her rules. And for that, I was truly grateful.

****

Even though I knew the true depths of her amoral wickedness, her evil wantonness, her raw anger, I also knew she could reward to the best of her ability. She could be generous and when it was simply normal sex between us (I never thought that possible but it did happen very frequently) she went a long way to demonstrate the actress within her – and have absolutely no doubt she was an Oscar standard performer.

We would finish a love making session and she would express her undying love for me and she would say things such as, "I want to walk in fields of green with you. I want to walk with you in Elysium, my Emperor, my Roman Emperor, my Lord Gaius Caligula. Let us deprave ourselves in front of Rome and visit the darkest recesses of our corruption. Let us teach all Caligulans how disgusting and perverted and utterly immoral we can be."

I would watch eagerly and wait as she stripped and moved in rhythm to Bolero or George Thorogood and The Destroyers as they hit the beat of Bad to the Bone or Roxy Music singing Let's Stick Together, Reg Presley and The

Troggs singing Wild Thing. Yes, Susie loved music with a sexy beat and she knew how to use it.

Oh God but she sent me wild with eager passion when she did these things. But it didn't change my feelings for her. There was no sudden forgiveness or reconciliation. If there was going to be that, I had to be certain the fits of jealous rage would be gone for ever. And how on earth was I ever going to be certain of that? If it had been possible for her to dispense with her dark side, we could have ended up having a near perfect relationship. But it was not to be.

Yes, she was bad to the bone alright. She was evil and perverted and immoral and possessed a fury beyond anything I had ever seen in any woman. It reached the stage where I was becoming frightened of her. On several occasions after the last violent incident, she refused to listen to the safe word and on those occasions, she really did physically (and mentally if the truth be known) hurt me: once to the extent that I came into the office one morning on elbow crutches (again); she had hurt me that much. Again, I feigned a pulled muscle in my back.

"It must be some muscle you pulled," one guy said, "because you look like you took a real whuppin'."

He never realised how close to the truth he was.

She would also refuse to say the safe word and when I refused to go any further (either because I thought she had had enough or I fetched blood) she would fly into a violent rage until I continued.

Once, when I absolutely refused point blank to go any further, she grabbed the violet wand from me, upped the voltage and shoved it inside of her again and again until she multi-orgasmed and when she became so physically tired of it, she could do it no more.

Yes, she frightened me. I was afraid she might kill

me and I was afraid she might also kill herself. Things had to be brought to a close.

****

By the very nature of humankind, some relationships must inevitably come to an end. Some survive years of problems, while others falter as soon as a spark of love or desire is ignited. Love affairs either survive for many years or they quickly fall apart and fizzle out like a Chinese firecracker. It is part and parcel of human nature.

The lowering of the heat of love in our affair was at first so small it could hardly be noticed but I felt the worm of dissatisfaction crawling in the deepest recesses of my thoughts. Eventually, Susie detected it (as she was bound to because somewhere inside of her there was an over-sensitive emotion detector) and the immediate result, her first reaction, was something totally unexpected.

"What's wrong, Glen?" she said after a 'normal' session of making love (which was over all too quickly).

And I came straight out with what was on my mind; there was no premium in delaying the inevitable or trying to hoodwink her by telling her untruths.

"I'm not going to lie to you, Susie, but I'm not happy about the way our relationship is going."

"You never mentioned anything before."

"No, I didn't and that was because I was afraid of what your reaction might be. No, I'll go further than that – I was frightened, scared of what your reaction *would* be. When you lose your temper, you sink to such depths of fury, I don't know how to handle it.

"Supposing my car really breaks down or I get involved in a road accident. What if you see me talking to one of my female colleagues at the office if I accidentally bump into her when we are out shopping? What if something happens to a member of my family again. I may be in the aftershock of a divorce but that does not negate any responsibility I may have for them. I can't run that risk again.

"That one time it happened, you physically and mentally hurt me. More than that, you practically frightened me to death. You must think about this before we continue our relationship any further. Think about it very seriously."

She said nothing, simply rolled over and slept.

The next morning, we hardly spoke; not at breakfast (which was just coffee and a croissant), not on the journey to the ferry and hardly on the ferry itself. It was only when we went our separate ways at the Manhattan Terminal she said, "I'll call you sometime. Don't cut me out completely. We can work things out. I can change."

"I'm sorry, Susie. If it had been a normal relationship, we could have gone on to who knows where. I just...I don't...I think we should give ourselves a cooling off period. We could have gone on together for whoever knows how long. But there was little that was normal about our relationship. It has a cancerous growth firmly embedded in it and I don't know how to stop it from growing."

"Okay, Glen. I'll call you sometime."

"Yes, call me." I was so surprised she was so conciliatory.

And we went our separate ways.

****

But it lasted just two weeks. She called me at the office almost every day for a few minutes chat and when it wasn't the office, it was my apartment.

The next time we went to her house on Staten Island, there was very definitely something wrong with the atmosphere. It was cold (and it was a warm spring day) and stale. The place smelled of rainy dampness. It was creepy. It could have been my imagination, but no, it was as if the atmosphere of the place was decaying before me.

So, over the next six weeks, until the complete breakdown of our relationship, we continued to meet at my apartment.

Yes, it was most definitely declining. The change in her was subtle at first; tired-looking eyes, darkening patches under her eyes, listlessness in her daily life, and it was like she was being drained of her life force by a vampire, slowly sucking the blood from her, but when she wanted physical love – or what she passed as physical love – (she was never really interested in the philosophical side of love – it was all physical with Susie; all physical or absolutely nothing) or when she wanted to give it, she was her 'normal' self and the actress within her had to take a rain check, but the animal lust within her never quite dead.

And after six weeks or so, a metamorphosis began to form. She tried to win me back by attempting the philosophical side of love but it was never going to work with her. I doubt if she had ever explored the philosophical side of love and she was too far gone, too immersed in her Caligulan depravity, to be a better person. She didn't realise her attempts were so amateurish and thus she continued on a downward slide.

She tried composing Sen Ryu (a branch of Haiku which concentrates on the human self as opposed to Haiku which concentrates purely on nature). She sent me several via my E Mail account, or left written ones around my apartment when she visited. There was no poet within her and they were not very good efforts. They had no skill, no structure. She wrote things like:

I kneel before you

My Emperor, my master

See my tears fall down

…and

I am your servant

I prostrate myself for you

Your manhood is king

…and

My tears flow freely

And my broken heart will die

If you forsake me

…and

Give me orgasm

I am naked before you

Be on heat for me

That last one sounded as if it had been written from sheer desperation and it continued in this vein.

I crave your manhood

Between my so eager lips

And my teeth to bite

...and

I deprave myself

And you reject all of me

Whip me one more time

...and these two I found particularly disturbing...

My life force going

Nothing left in me to live

A leap of faith – yes!

…and

I fall through the air

I fall to eternity

My destiny – Hell!

She attempted these in a rather amateurish way: she hadn't quite got the full meaning of the language structure of Haiku or Sen Ryu. But Susie never gave up on something she wanted and she wanted to express her feelings for me through the Sen Ryu she kept composing. But she was far too immersed in rules (her rules?) to see that it takes more than rules to compose ancient Japanese poetry. It takes a mindset of beautiful proportions which she never possessed.

But I wouldn't have any of it. She was too far gone and neither of us could force a recovery. I no longer loved her and she was too blinded by her wild passion to see it. She would lie in bed at weekends – and maybe not turn up at her office – until the mid morning or early afternoon because she was too mentally drained to get up and face the day.

And then the metamorphosis began to deepen.

****

The gifts started as unimportant little trinkets / things / doohickeys that were really unimportant to me but not to her. I would just say, "Oh thanks," put it to one side or in a drawer and then forget about it. And then the items would become better quality and more expensive – and more noticeable. I didn't like to tell her to stop buying me these little gewgaws in case she became offended and vented her fury on me and I felt that fury just below the surface of her.

But when the items became really expensive (the diamond cufflinks, the 22 carat tie pin, the Rolex watch, the expensive fragrances blah blah blah) I felt I had to take her to one side and speak to her seriously about it.

Susie had been too demanding, too…creepy, too physically destructive in her deepest desires to be physically hurt but it was the mental side of her which was hurting and that could never be used as a reason for me to stay with her. I knew then I had to finish it permanently. I didn't know how I was going to do it and on a Sunday morning in early June 2008, I was rehearsing in my mind how I would broach the subject when she turned up unannounced at my apartment.

The metamorphosis, it appeared, had mutated into something truly monstrous. She had cried so much that the surrounding area of her eyes were stained black with her mascara and the tears ran down her cheeks in black semi-liquid rivulets. And her hair and lipstick were a mess and it made her look like Medusa the Gorgon. The complexion of her face was deathly pale and it made her look so ill, so…so ghostly, as if all of the blood had drained from her.

She was naked beneath her raincoat and before she threw the coat aside, she took from the deep inside pocket several of her S and M items – a couple of whips and a riding crop.

She fell to her knees before me and implored me to hurt her, to whip her, until she bled and screamed and her intensity was such that she drove herself to uncontrollable tears, she was so desperate to reach down to the depths of her amoral corruption and drag me down with her.

I pulled her back on her feet and looked into her black eyes. "This has to stop, Susie. I'm getting too deep into this and you are out of control. What you want me to do is utterly insane. Stop it. Stop it now!"

She sank to her knees again and implored me to stay with her.

"Stay with me, Glen. I worship you like you are a

pagan god. I cannot be without you. My life is nothing without you. It is nothing, nothing, NOTHINGGGG!!!"

It was a pathetic attempt and I felt deeply embarrassed. She wept like a child who has lost her puppy dog and she would not, could not stop.

I picked her up from her knees and I almost fell again under her spell when she said, "Glen – pleeeeeaaase!! I can change. I know how to change. I can be a very nice person to you. Believe me I can."

But for an instant, she let down her protective shield and I could look inside her and see all of the dirty, scummy, unspeakable degeneracy of her being and all of her rottenness was visible to the naked eye. I could see her as we were making love one night and while she straddled me, she flogged herself until she bled. Her search for that ultimate peak of lust was insatiable. And I couldn't fall again. Not ever.

"Susie, just go. Make yourself decent and go. You have to give me time to think about this, our entire relationship. But this, what you do, what you want me to do, is not what I want. Not any more. Just go."

And she did. She put on her raincoat and walked out of the door without a word, without bothering to dry her black mascara stained tears, without bothering to adjust her makeup or her hair or her lipstick. She looked a physical mess and mentally, she was wrecked. She was not physically or mentally capable of changing. She was too far gone.

Whenever Susie came to my apartment, she would use her car. She would leave Staten Island via Interstate 278, into Brooklyn and out via Interstate 478 through the Brooklyn Battery Tunnel and into Manhattan. My apartment block was a building of fifty floors on the Upper West Side. On a good day, I could see the Intrepid Museum on Pier 86 at West 46th Street.

I watched her get in her car thirty floors below and drive away.

I made black coffee.

Damn, I didn't want her to come back again today because she had left behind her pack of cigarillos and her gold cigarette lighter. So I took one and smoked it while tasting the black coffee. The two together were relaxing and I got to thinking I might take in a ball game or something in Central Park so I put on my jacket and left the apartment.

As I unlocked my car, my cell phone rang. I answered it. It was Susie.

She said, "Look up to the roof, Glen."

And then the phone went dead.

I looked up and saw her standing on the lip of the roof fifty floors above me. Two things left her hands: a knife and her cell phone. She let go of them together. Then a few seconds later, she leaned over and launched herself off the roof and began hurtling toward the ground. Her cell phone hit the ground first and shattered into a hundred pieces before me and followed almost instantaneously by the knife. The blade broke through the impact. Seconds later, Susie hit the roof of my car with a sickening crunch.

The police found her raincoat on the roof of my apartment building. The autopsy later revealed that she didn't launch herself from the roof but slit her own throat; then she toppled forward off the roof and was already dying.

****

Did Susie believe she would never fall in love and have a normal life as others do? What true effort does it take? Thus, she substituted a happily married life – or a long term relationship – for the excitement her depraved and voracious sex life would offer her. I'm no psychologist, but that is what it seemed like to me. However, one must never pass an opinion on someone one does not really know and when my knowledge of Susie began to increase, I began to understand why men shied away from her soon after the beginning of a relationship. Perhaps I should have followed their path – I had had enough opportunity – but I was ever willing to take a chance and I chose a different path instead.

I scorned Susie; at least that is the way she must have seen it and dead or not, she was not going to let me get away with it because a couple of weeks after she threw herself off the roof of my apartment building, something, a coldness, an awareness, a very deeply disturbing atmosphere came into my apartment early one Sunday morning and it came with the intention of remaining.

It felt like Susie. It even smelled like Susie (who could possibly mistake that exquisitely luscious perfume of hers – only she could wear Chanel No 5 like it had been personally tailored for her). It was Susie and Susie wanted revenge and come hell or high water, she was going to get what she wanted.

Vermont: 1938

And this is where I think it all started. I can't decide whether it was one single event which brought about the decline of Susie's family – and in the end, Susie herself – or if it was a combination of things, events, people. I haven't the time or the inclination to delve any deeper and go into the philosophical whys and wherefores of when this happened or where that happened or why this or that should be. I'll leave that to the experts. Mayhap, Professor Weissman, you might be interested; it might give you a few clues as to what made me tick then and certainly what makes me tick now.

Well, professor, here it is, my interpretation of the diaries. Perhaps you ought to read them yourself. There is nothing quite like insight.

****

Heaven was a day in Fall when the scent of fallen and bronzed leaves was carried on a warm south westerly breeze across the rich and prosperous farmlands of Vermont to lap at the shores of Lake Champlain. The mid-morning sun was unusually warm and pleasant to the feel of one's skin and enhanced the white walls and red tiled roofs of the farm houses dotted about the Champlain Valley, and when *Rock of Ages* echoed from Springwater Baptist Church on this Sunday of October 16 1938, peace and contentment reigned supreme over all.

The hymn, a firm favourite with the small but utterly devoted congregation of farmers, their wives and children, was being sung as a prayer to the good Lord above so that He may ease the burden of their brothers and sisters in the mid-west who were still suffering the deprivation and aftermath of the Great Depression and whose vast prairie farmlands, along with countless smallholdings run by the poorest of people, were degenerating still into so much dry, sterile and utterly useless dust, while those in Vermont were basking in a world of plenty, where the soil was deep and rich, the grass green and lush, where the milk of the dairy herds was to die for and the harvest of maple syrup and honey from the numerous hives was enjoying another record breaking season.

When the hymn had finished, the Reverend Ethan Saul continued with the closing part of his sermon.

"And the Lord God of Abraham said unto Pharaoh through Moses: I shall visit plagues upon you and your people and strike ye dead!

"And, brothers and sisters, it is happening again. History is repeating itself. Those in power, those in government, will tell you it is nothing more than a freak of nature and that it will pass and when it does, all will be right with the world.

"They tell us we must wait to see if it changes for the better. But it is God alone who controls all in creation and it is He who has brought this great plague down upon our brothers and sisters in the mid-west because of their sins, their vileness, their unceasing lowering into debauchery and lust and strong drink and loose women and base wickedness!

"It is as if the great plains of the mid-west are turned into Sodom and Gomorrah, those twin cities of evil and godlessness!

"Oh Lord God of Abraham smite thine enemies and cleanse the sins of Sodom and Gomorrah from the hearts and souls of thy sons and daughters that they may once again be clean of mind, body and soul."

They made fun of him in their homes and his hellfire and brimstone method of preaching (but never to his face or in the presence of his wife Pandora, or her daughter, Athenia: the congregation were too hypocritical for that) because they did not believe all of this nonsense he spouted every Sunday morning. They believed in a loving and all-forgiving God, not a God full of vengeance. But to maintain the good Reverend's required standards, his own *status quo*, they were all ears and attention at Sunday morning worship. But what truly frightened them about Ethan Saul was the fact that he was a true religious fanatic. He would have no other faith but his own and as far as he was concerned, any other faith was a blasphemy in the eyes of his God.

His congregation were true God-fearing people but at the same time, the God they liked to believe in, regardless of what Ethan Saul tried to drum into them, was good, kind and benevolent. In this modern day and age, there was no place for a vengeful God and in this, the happiest of all farming communities, there was also little room for Bible-thumping hypocrites. They simply went along with the Reverend and pretended to play his game, feeling that since he was human like the rest of them, he had his faults and thus, he at least deserved their devotion to religious duty, if not their respect.

They would rather believe in the richness and productivity of the land, brought on by the sweat of their brows and the calluses on their hands. They believed in the goodness of people – neighbours, friends, relations. Yes, God had His place within these hills and valleys and they would talk to Him betimes when they were troubled or when they wished to give thanks for the end of a hard day's work or a good harvest.

To them, Reverend Ethan Saul was merely a rusted tool whose usefulness as a credible Christian guide within the community had long since faded. He came across to them as a crackpot Bible thumper whose place was really in the dustbowls of the mid-west or the seething southern states of the true Bible belt. But not in this green and pleasant land.

But they knew things about Ethan Saul. One thing for sure, they knew he was having a full physical relationship with an unmarried woman who lived at Shelburne Bay along Route 7 and just a little shy of Burlington. Mayhap Pandora Saul knew about it too and mayhap she did not because she looked so innocent of the wickedness of the world and of her husband. But no one was courageous enough to face her with the truth. Not a one of them was so sure of the facts that he or she could face the Reverend with them and none of the clucking hens and gaggling geese of the women's church groups wanted to face Pandora Saul with the truth either. Talking about it behind their backs seemed to be justified for the time being and if she already knew, as like as not she might tell them to mind their own goddamn business, and if she didn't know, not a one of them would like to be the one to break her heart with the full story. The truth of it was none of them knew of the sinful depths Reverend Ethan Saul could sometimes sink to or of the solid iron will which lived within Pandora Saul.

But on the surface of this fine Harvest Festival Sunday, Heaven in all of its glory shone down on the valley on this peaceful day and on this, the third Sunday of October 1938, when the service was over, Reverend Ethan Saul stood outside his church with his wife - she a small looking woman who looked as if she could be blown away by the wispiest of light breezes and seemed as if she hadn't a care in the world (hence, the almost permanent smile on her face). But below the angelic looking surface, there seethed a rage like a volcano longing to erupt. She was more than aware that her husband's sermon on the evils of temptation through drink, gambling and loose women had probably again been fired by his own weaknesses.

She knew of the amount of whiskey he drank and in his drunkenness, he would fly into almost uncontrollable rages. She knew of the unmarried woman who lived in

Shelburne Bay, but what she did not know (merely suspected) was that for several years, he had been abusing his own daughter. He had denied on oath to the Holy Bible that he had not done this evil thing and she received the same denial when she spoke to Athenia on the several occasions she had broached the subject with her.

He had noticed that from the age of fourteen years, she had been rapidly growing into a woman, a real woman, with all of a woman's natural curves and Pandora had noticed the way Ethan looked at Athenia when he had been drinking heavily. She could not fail to see the wildness of lustful fire in his eyes, the lecherous looks he gave her and though she could never prove anything, she took precautions for Athenia by dressing her in unfashionable and mundanely coloured clothes, banning her from wearing makeup and by encouraging constant reading of her Bible. She also vehemently forbade her any association whatsoever with boys, whomsoever he should be. The exception to the rule was Tomas de Francia, her fiancé and intended husband to be in a carefully arranged marriage between two wealthy families.

They shook the hands of each of their flock as they emerged from the church, engaged in a few brief lines of conversation with each and closed each conversation by requesting their presence at the Harvest Festival supper that evening.

After the last of his congregation had left, Reverend Saul, who always liked to open up his church on a Sunday morning and thus permitted his wife and Athenia to follow at a later time, said to his wife, "I noticed a certain member of our congregation was missing this morning."

"I don't understand," she said. "I never count how many attend because all seats always seem to be taken."

"I meant to say the choir was missing a valued and

sweet angel's voice. A number of the congregation, and indeed the choirmaster, have remarked upon it this day and I could not give them an answer because I had none to give."

Pandora Saul looked mystified.

"Athenia," he prompted. "Where is she?"

"Oh yes. She wasn't feeling too well this morning so I told her she should stay at home."

"And what is 'not feeling too well' supposed to mean? If all of my congregation gave the same excuse, there would be a half empty church for me to preach to on most Sunday mornings. If people are unwell and a physician or a cure cannot immediately be found, who else better to turn to but the Lord our God in Heaven above? She will attend the service this evening and without fail."

"Only if she is well enough to attend. Women do have their problems once a month and Athenia is no exception."

"It is nothing which cannot be banished by getting down upon her knees to pray to the Lord. She will attend the service this evening. I hope I make myself clear."

"Yes, Ethan, you do. But you will have to bring her. And in the car. I don't wish to walk back home along dark country lanes. In a few minutes, I shall be chairing a Harvest Festival committee meeting. We have to finalise matters for this evening and if you don't get going, you will meet yourself coming back."

Yes, such was a heavenly Sunday in Springwater.

****

Hell was a day when Athenia Susanne Saul, the only child of Reverend Ethan and Mrs. Pandora Lillian Saul, turned further the key to the box of woes her mother had inserted long ago and opened it further to the world. It was a day on which she lied to her mother by feigning illness and thus being discovered by her father in their barn, worse the wear for drink, butt naked and cavorting with Frankie Miller, one of Ethan Saul's farmhands (who should also have attended the Sunday morning service – he having an almost perfect bass singing voice and therefore being an essential part of the choir).

Ethan Saul had walked the three miles to church: he refused to take the car since it gave him no exercise. Cars, according to him, were for long journeys and thus he had left the red 1931 Lasalle Town Sedan in the barn which he used as a garage. George and Jennifer Schilling had collected Pandora in their horse drawn open top Brougham and taken her to Springwater Baptist Church to worship.

Ethan Saul took the walk home as an excuse to drink heavily from the bottle of sour mash whiskey he had with him and it lay in his knapsack next to his Bible. He was of a bad temper on this day and the sour mash made it even worse, made it more dangerous by the fact that he was obliged to attend the Harvest Festival supper as opposed to visiting Miss Frances Montpelier in Shelburne Bay just a few minutes south of Burlington and on the peaceful shores of Lake Champlain.

He was seething now as he walked along the driveway to the house and wondering why his barn door was open. He knew it was not any of the farm hands because he strictly forbad any work to be done on the sabbath day, apart from the essential tasks of milking and feeding the cattle, and all of that had been done earlier in the morning at just before sun up and finishing just an hour or so after. All, except Athenia and Frankie Miller had then attended Springwater Baptist Church for the Sunday morning service.

But then he remembered Athenia had not attended the Sunday morning service and was at home and when he remembered that neither had he seen Frankie Miller in the choir, his drink-befuzzled mind began to put two and two together and allowed his seething anger to come to the surface. He had seen Frankie Miller giving his daughter the eye and it was almost as if Ethan could read his thoughts. He was lusting after her, he thought, and this made him angrier still.

He reached the barn door and walked quietly in. He heard noises coming from the interior of the car, squeals and laughing, silly girlish giggling and the kind of language he associated with the gutter.

"Come on, Frankie, come and fuck me," he heard Athenia say. "Come on, you know you want to." And more girlish squeals.

Ethan Saul took up a horsewhip and carefully and quietly approached the car. As quick as a lightning flash, he snatched open the rear door of the sedan.

And then a startled squeal of, "Oh my God, daddy!"

And a "Jesus Christ!" from Frankie Miller.

They were both naked and Frankie was in a state of extreme excitement with Athenia's long and slender fingers wrapped around him.

Ethan Saul grabbed Frankie by his long, unshorn hair, dragged him out of the car and snapped the horsewhip across his butt three times in rapid succession and very hard.

"That is for taking the name of the Lord thy God in vain," and he laid the horsewhip across him another three times at which Frankie yelped in severe pain.

"And that is for doing things with my daughter neither of you should be doing until she has taken a husband – which I guarantee, Francis John Miller, will never be you. Now get off my land, you cavorting little bastard, and run as far west as you can because I guarantee one more thing. If I find you have penetrated her, I will have you arrested on a charge of statutory rape and thrown into the very darkest and deepest jail I can find."

Frankie pulled himself free and ran. He ran for his life, dressing as he ran. He had his freedom for eight days until he was arrested in Fair Haven, Rutland County. He was initially charged with statutory rape since Athenia was still two weeks shy of her eighteenth birthday and he was twenty six.

******

If there had been eight deadly sins instead of seven, Reverend Ethan Saul would have been soundly guilty of the eighth – hypocrisy! He had been molesting his daughter since she had started to become a true woman but had always stopped short of penetration. Even before these secret sessions with his growing daughter, he would get down on his knees and pray to the Lord for guidance in this his hour of need, to help him turn his face away from this sinful lust.

"Swear an oath on the good book," he would say to her, "that if you ever mention one word of this to any living man or woman, I will bring down upon you such a wrath of God you will pray for the kindest mercy He can give you."

And she complied because in her innocence of the wicked ways of the world and of Ethan Saul, she was utterly afraid of him and his immense strength and what she thought he might be capable of doing. Thus, she endured his wandering hands whenever the need took him, which often was when his anger reddened his face and the whiskey made his breath stink like the devil's front door.

"You goddamned and cursed spawn of Jezebel!" he said as he dragged her by her hair from the car.

"Daddy, I swear we were not doing anything bad."

"Nothing bad? Damn you for your evil. You were naked before him and drunk from the wanton partaking of strong liquor! You are worse than the whores of Sodom and Gomorrah and your punishment shall be swift and sure!"

"No, daddy! Please! We were not doing - "

"Be silent, damn you! I'm going to chastise the hide off you and make certain you learn humility and respect and to put the vile temptations of Eve behind you!"

"No, daddy! No! No - !"

And he struck her with the flat of his powerful hand across her face with such force, she was knocked to the ground and remained unconscious for several minutes.

When she came to, she felt strange; not strange as being faint from the blow but strange below, in between her legs and she hurt in her most private place. She felt the pain of soreness, of being torn and there was a warm, sticky liquid oozing from her. She felt - ? Violated.

But it was nothing like the pain of the horsewhip across her rear as Ethan Saul struck her and at the same time, quoted from the Bible.

"Watch and pray that ye enter not into temptation: the spirit is indeed willing but the flesh is weak."

He struck her again.

"And almost all things are by the Lord purged with blood; and without the shedding of blood, there is no remission of sin."

And a third time.

"He that spareth his rod hateth his son: but he that loveth him chasteneth him betimes."

And a fourth time.

"They shall not drink wine with a song; strong drink shall be bitter to them that drink it."

And a fifth time.

"Behold, how good and how pleasant it is for brethren to dwell together in unity."

And he grasped at her hair and pulled her head back. "In unity, you evil whore! You sinful daughter of Eve! Not when you are cavorting and depraving yourself and naked with the lowest of the low!"

And he struck her a sixth time.

"Having therefore these promises, let us cleanse ourselves from all filthiness of the flesh and spirit and perfecting holiness in the fear of God."

And though his anger had taken the three mile walk home to grow, it was gone in almost an instant. It was as if a light had been switched on to bring him out of the darkness into the brightness of day. But the light of day revealed his vile sin. He fell to his knees and prayed for the redemption of this his most wicked of sins.

Athenia dressed quickly and sneaked away, fearful he might do other things to her. She went into the house and locked the door to her bedroom. Some time later, he came and knocked and spoke kind words to her, but she refused to open the door. He tried the door several times but she said through it, "If you break the door down and get in here, I'll tell momma of everything that happened. Don't you dare ever touch me like that again. Don't you ever touch me with your hands. Don't you ever dare come near me again and believe this, daddy. For what you have done to me today, I hope one day to be able to piss and spit on your grave."

Now he was enraged by her words and he kicked and punched at the door several times but he couldn't gain entry. And he could do nothing more; not now, not ever.

****

On Harvest Sunday of October 16 1938, Reverend Ethan Saul raped his daughter two weeks before her eighteenth birthday and six months before her arranged marriage to Tomas de Francia and no matter how much over the coming weeks he prayed to the Lord for forgiveness and redemption of his wicked and lustful ways, his heart remained empty and his soul as black as the deepest night.

Six years later and on the day he put a noose around his neck and hung himself, he realised the rape of his daughter had been the day the Lord had abandoned him completely and utterly.

****

Athenia was tall for her age and quite attractive; a proper young woman who, had she been given the opportunity, would have broken many more hearts than that of Frankie Miller, who was now languishing in a prison cell and awaiting trial. Word was out that there would be no trial by jury because he would be tried on a lesser charge of molestation. Juries meant publicity and Pandora Saul would have none of it. She had made contact with County Court Judge Oscar Rheinhardt and reminded him of certain things she knew.

She didn't attend the harvest supper and when Pandora made enquiries of her husband, he lied by telling her she was still indisposed. She left it at that until a couple of days later when she closely questioned her daughter on her continued moodiness.

****

It did not take a brilliant mind for Athenia to discover what had really happened, even though she had never discussed matters of relationships between man and woman with her mother. But it took her a couple of days to figure it out. She had her suspicions on the day it happened but she had to be certain of every detail. She had been unconscious and something evil had taken her. She knew it hadn't been Frankie because she stopped him before he could enter her (even though she had goaded him to do it) and she knew of everything (due again to her own encouragement of him) Frankie Miller had done. More importantly, she knew what he had not done.

Athenia could no longer hold back her fears and over the next half hour, she told her mother in every detail precisely what had happened on that day, both with Frankie Miller and her father.

"You were cavorting naked with a lousy farmhand?"

"Yes, mother, but we - "

"Shut up!" her mother said as she slapped her face. "Just answer my questions and if I once perceive you to be lying, I will lay you across this kitchen table and thrash the truth from you. Do you understand?"

"Yes, mother."

"Did penetration take place between you and Frankie Miller?"

"No, mother. But when daddy found me with him, he hit me and laid me unconscious. When I came to, I was draped over the picket fence and I felt – I felt as if I had been violated."

"By Frankie Miller?"

"No. I told you and I swear an oath on the good book it was not Frankie. It was daddy. Frankie was sent packing after daddy laid a horsewhip across him and it was daddy who raped me. For around four years now, he has been putting his hands all over me and each time he did it, he made me swear an oath I was never ever to tell anyone, but most of all you, about what we had done – what *he* had done!"

It seemed like ages before Pandora could fully understand what Athenia had told her. She felt sick to her stomach and she desperately struggled to fight back her tears as much as she possibly could and really struggled to control her rising anger.

She sat opposite Athenia at the kitchen table with her face as blank as blank could be, giving nothing away and not permitting Athenia to know what she was thinking. And then without warning, she slapped Athenia's face so hard, she knocked her off her chair.

"You evil, conniving little slut. This would not have happened with your father – or with Frankie Miller – had you not lied to me on Sunday morning just so that you could cavort naked and do abhorrent things with that low life, shiftless, no account farmhand and committing vile sin with him. How could you? How could you do this to me? You are worse than the Whore of Babylon. Now get out of my sight. Go to your room until I decide what must be done."

****

It had been arranged for some considerable time that Athenia would marry Tomas de Francia, a law student at New York Law School and the son of a wealthy immigrant Mexican / Spanish family in the district of Rutland County and who could trace their Spanish roots back to the time of Tomas de Torquemada. They also had a younger child, a daughter, Emilia.

It was a carefully planned and arranged marriage in the true sense of the term. Pandora, the true wealth within her family and the second last in line, had openly encouraged the de Francia family (and Tomas) that marriage to her daughter would ensure the solidity of both family fortunes and add to the land acquisitions and financial stability of both.

Pandora knew from the very beginning that it was more of a business deal than a marriage: love between Athenia and Tomas didn't come into the procedure and who should know better than Pandora Saul? Her own marriage had been a loveless waste of time almost from the very beginning.

****

Two months later, Pandora Saul took the opportunity of her husband's absence (she guessed he had gone to see that woman in Shelburne Bay) to have a serious talk with her daughter and to give her advice whether she needed it or not.

"Athenia, I am going to ask you a direct question and I want a truthful answer. In fact, I want truthful answers to a number of questions. Am I very clearly understood?"

"Yes, mother."

"Are you pregnant? Because I have noticed your morning sickness over the past week."

"Yes, mother, I think I am. Neither did my period happen this month."

"I'll ask you again a question I asked you a while back and think carefully before you answer. When you were caught with Frankie Miller, had penetration of any sort taken place?"

"No, mother. I swear it on the good book. May I burn in Hell if I'm lying. I wouldn't let him do anything like that to me. He wanted to but I wouldn't let him. I only intended for us to fool around and not get serious about anything."

"He said at his trial you invited him to do it."

"I was just teasing him, mother, and I never meant anything to go any further than it did with him."

"Did any of his fluid come into contact with you? His fluid from down below?"

"No, mother. Things didn't even reach that far. We had both just got undressed when daddy caught us."

"Is it Tomas de Francia's child?"

"No, mother. Apart from the occasional kiss, we have never, ever been intimate."

"Have you not lain with Tomas?"

"No, mother."

"And you are certain beyond any possible shadow of a doubt it was your father who ravaged you?"

"Yes, mother. I swear on my life it was him."

Pandora already knew most of the answers but she felt she had to ask one final time before relating her final decisions to her daughter.

"Alright, I'm satisfied you are telling the truth in all of these matters and these are the decisions I have made. These decisions will salvage our family's reputation and your own should it become known in other quarters that certain things have been going on. I cannot speak for your father, though I say without any regret whatsoever I hope he burns in eternal hellfire for the utter shame he has brought upon this house.

"Have you told Tomas of what your father did?"

"No, mother. I have told no one."

"Then you will never tell him. I have made a firm decision on this matter and it will be for your own good and the good of your future marriage. I can arrange for you to have an abortion."

Athenia's jaw dropped as she heard her mother say

this.

"Oh don't look so shocked, child. It is the very best thing to do under the circumstances. How otherwise would you explain a pregnancy on your wedding day, a pregnancy which is six months old and when Tomas knows he is not the father? And if you gave birth to your father's child, it would be your brother or your sister and it will call you mama. Witless idiot that he is betimes, Tomas does not deserve that.

"The lady I shall take you to see has done this a number of times before when a pregnancy would prove to be deeply embarrassing and she guarantees the process will be painless. Trust in her and trust in me. This is the right decision to make. I am only thinking of your future. And one thing is for certain; you must never tell Tomas of what your father did. No one must ever know. Do you understand everything I have said to you?"

"Yes, mother, but Frankie will go to prison for something he didn't do."

"Frankie Miller knew according to the laws of this state you were under age. Let it be a lesson to him. And you will maintain complete silence about him as well.

"And that is the way it shall remain. Arrangements have been made with County Court Judge Oscar Rheinhardt that the case and sentencing will be heard in private and without a jury. He is to be arraigned on a lesser charge of molestation. He will serve two years and after that, he will be released. But you will never see him again. Certain unsavoury things are known about Judge Oscar Rheinhardt and I make it my business to know. Knowledge is power. Never, ever forget that.

"And the night before Frankie Miller's trial, I will rehearse you in the evidence you will present to the court. I don't care a damn about Frankie Miller and he is going to get what is coming to him. Listen to me, child, in all things because I know what is going to be best for you.

"After the wedding, you will never see your father again. He will be leaving this house and I don't want him back. But that is not for you to tell him. Just keep away from him as much as you possibly can. We will see for how long his slut in Shelburne Bay tolerates his everyday presence. He has been a burden to me and I want shut of him.

"I want you to have no further contact with your father after the wedding. The last time he will ever have any physical contact with you is when he will walk you along the aisle in church to your future husband. And I shall be keeping a very close eye on him until then. I have Reverend Bonham from Burlington parish to conduct the ceremony. After that, as far as you are concerned, your father will cease to exist. I do not wish for this conversation or any of his scandals to go beyond the four walls of this room."

****

If Pandora had her time over again, it would not have been Ethan Saul who would have taken her for a wife. Her father had branded Lucas Richmond a '...Catholic heathen son of a bitch...' and flatly refused Pandora permission to marry him. She had lain with him on several occasions and he was the love of her life. Her tears were long, heavy and bitter when she told him of her father's decision. She told him on the day before Thanksgiving Day and on Thanksgiving Day, November 29 1917, he enlisted with the army and after basic training, he left Vermont to go and fight the war in Europe. He came back in a box eight months later and was buried with full military honours.

And even then and ever since, she sometimes shed tears for him and always in her deepest and most private thoughts, she mourned his loss. She also regularly tended his grave at Calvary Cemetery in Rutland. She did so quite openly and unashamedly. Whether Ethan knew about it or not, she didn't know, and neither did she care.

She inherited her father's wealth but not until he had forced her into a sour marriage in 1918 with Ethan Saul, a Baptist religious fanatic and firebrand from Jackson, Tennessee. He was virtually penniless when he came to Vermont but when there was hard work to be done, he used the sweat of his brow and the muscle of his back to get it done. He kept up the quality of the farm's herd of Jersey and Guernsey cattle and continued it as a fine dairy herd which was the envy of the county (but without Pandora's and her father's money, he would have been next to nothing). But still she could not find it in herself to love him. Lucas Richmond was always at the forefront of her memory and remained so for the rest of her life.

****

There was no historic family reason for Ethan Saul to be lean and tall. It simply happened that at the age of sixteen, when his father almost beat the life out of him and threw him out on to the street for hanging around with those '…goddamned religious people…' he just started to grow. Perhaps it was the sudden relief of leaving an unhappy home where a drunken and violent father had reigned supreme. His mother was a small and wispy, weak looking woman, an Irish immigrant from parents of the potato famine, who simply tolerated the frequent black eyes and cut lips, the kickings and the beatings with a leather belt. Her only child, Ethan, tolerated the same beatings but said enough was enough when his father finally beat his mother to death. For that, he kept an appointment with the hangman's rope in Tennessee State Prison. He died cursing his wife and son.

Ethan took up permanent residence with the River Jordan Travelling Baptist Show because he had found solace in its religion and it kept him from bad memories of his violent father. He later enrolled at a small Baptist college where he rapidly gained his pastorship and gained a pastor's position (a lucrative one to him, as it turned out) in Springwater, Vermont. He worked hard on John Weston's farm to supplement his meagre income but the fire that burned in his heart and soul was that of religious mania. The flame of hellfire and damnation burned in his eyes and his thin wiry arms and legs carried much strength to bear the burden of his heavy work.

After the long and painful birth of their daughter, Athenia Susanne, in the Fall of 1920, Pandora denied him any further acts of physical love and when he complained to her about this denial of his conjugal rights, she told him to '...go and fuck the cows in the field if you are that desperate but don't you dare ever lay hands on me again.' She had the child by him because she did not want him to inherit any part of her wealth: it would now all go to her daughter.

And thus he took to womanising which she had no real objection to, providing he kept these things where they should be kept (at the very least, Pandora blamed herself for his womanising but she thought him no less a hypocrite for it when he spouted against it in his sermons). What Pandora objected to was the fact that he flaunted what they both knew – that women were attracted to him and the fact that the clucking hens of the Baptist congregation of Springwater tattle-taled about Ethan's extra-marital affairs and in consequence, laughed at Pandora behind her back. But as she told her daughter, '...knowledge is power...' and she knew things about some of them they would rather not be made public knowledge.

She had gained this knowledge by hiring a private detective out of Boston to dig for dirt on certain members of Ethan's congregation (the information on County Court Judge Oscar Rheinhardt had come as a welcome bonus) and she was not found wanting.

When she learned of the rape of her daughter by Ethan, she chose her own moment to confront him about it.

****

The wedding was a good event on a good day. Sunday March 5 1939 was an unusually warm day for the time of year but the congregation was not aware of the coldness emanating from the family of Reverend Ethan Saul. The family smiles were forced. Their conversation with the guests was forced but polite and Tomas de Francia was in total ignorance of the condition his wife had been in: furthermore, he was totally ignorant of the fact that she had had an abortion and this fact he would never know. But if truth be known, he wouldn't know a virgin if she threw herself at him butt naked and provided those who did know, kept their mouths very firmly shut.

Two things were uppermost in Pandora Saul's mind: firstly, she knew Athenia on this day was as happy as she was ever going to be and secondly, by the early afternoon of the following day, her own marriage would be well and truly over, at least in name only.

The wedding festivities ended and Athenia and Tomas de Francia lost no time in taking to their marriage bed. Athenia gave herself up to her husband willingly. On the day he left to return to law school in the middle of April after the Easter semester, she told him she was pregnant. He was happy about the situation and blissfully unaware of the fact that this was not the first time she had been with child.

The rain which was forecast for the day of the wedding came the following day and it made the Monday look and feel as it was in the house where Ethan Saul and his wife resided.

****

"It is strange not having Athenia sitting with us at the breakfast table," Ethan Saul said to his wife.

"Yes it is. But it is also convenient."

She had in front of her a whiskey tumbler filled almost to the brim with the fiery liquid.

"Convenient? I don't understand and what are you doing with that glass of whiskey?"

She didn't answer the last question but said, "Convenient for the both of us to talk about certain things."

"I still don't understand."

"Well, Ethan Saul, Reverend Pastor of Springwater Baptist Church, let me enlighten you. God obviously will not so I guess He has left this most unsavoury of tasks to me."

"I wish you would explain. You are talking in riddles. Has it got anything to do with that whiskey in front of you? It is rather a large glass."

"There is only one riddle to solve here – why in the name of Christ Almighty did I ever put up with you and your lotharic ways for all of these years?"

"What are you talking about?"

"Don't act the innocent with me. I'm talking about all of the affairs you have had with other women over the years. The constant lies of telling me you were on parish business when what you were really doing was out somewhere fucking some other woman."

"Pandora! I will not tolerate the use of foul language in this house!"

"In case you had forgotten, husband of mine, this happens to be my home on my land. It is in my name and mine alone and on my death, all of my property and my money will go to Athenia. You won't get a cent. You haven't even got two cents to rub together in your damn pocket so if you want to hire a lawyer to contest my will, good luck in trying to find the money to pay for him. And they don't come cheap.

"And if in my home I wish to use the word 'fuck' then so what? If it means I have a glass of whiskey in front of me – and I may well have a dozen or so more by the time this day is over – so what? And you keep your hands off it. My whiskey in my home. It'll help give me the Dutch courage I need to tie up some loose ends of business today."

"Can't this wait? You don't appear to be in the right frame of mind to make any rational decisions."

"Frame of mind? And what frame of mind am I in? But let me tell you I am not drunk. I am so very sober you wouldn't believe how sober I am. I'll get drunk later when I'm on my own and regretting and cursing the day my daddy made me hitch up with you.

"But I can assure you I am in the right frame of mind to make the decisions I have to make. And it has to be today. No other day will do."

"Decisions? What decisions are you talking about?"

"The most important decisions of my life. Today, I am going to do precisely what I want to do. Do you think all the years we have been married I haven't noticed what has been going on?"

"Pandora, these women – they meant nothing. I know I have sinned and I have repented and - "

"Do not bring that religious garbage into this conversation! I've known about your womanising almost from the very first time you went galivanting across this county with your cock as stiff as an oak post! Do you think I'm so utterly stupid I don't notice these things? I've seen the way they look at you with those leering eyes, hoping for another fumble in the hayrick or under the oak tree at the top of some field. I know most of the families in Springwater know about your canoodling and they talk about it – but behind my back. They never had the goddamn guts to say anything to my face!

"Do you sense they are talking about you too? They do, you know. They say your sermons are hypocritical beyond belief because you commit every vile sin you rant and rave against.

"I know of my own foolishness in allowing your escapades to continue for all of these years. I know we are the subject of their whispered conversations, but then there is a sudden and embarrassed change of subject when I approach. Those two faced, back-stabbing, cackling and clucking hens. Who are they to talk about our private lives when I'll bet my last cent not a one of them knows what a good fucking feels like."

"What is your point, Pandora? I can mend my ways. I can change with the help of the good Lord - "

"The good Lord? The good Lord? Wherever He is, He certainly does not reside in this home! He has abandoned this home and left me to sort out the goddamn mess."

"I'm – I'm sorry, Pandora. I'm sorry I've brought so much trouble on this house."

"In more ways than one. I know about Frances Montpelier in Shelburne Bay and I know it has been going on for four years – and you have even cheated on her for God's sake! I wonder if the silly damned whore realises that?"

"She is not a whore! Do not call that woman a whore or I'll - "

"Or you will what? If she is fucking my husband, reputedly a man of the cloth and a Baptist minister, she is in my book a whore. So what are you going to do about it? All of this foul language and all of these accusations? Are you going to remove your leather belt and lay it across me? Or are you going to use a horsewhip like you did with Athenia six months gone?"

"I – I don't understand."

"Don't play the innocent with me. The hordes of women you have seduced I cannot and will not forgive but I will tolerate the pain of it because I suppose in a way it was me who drove you away from me and towards them. I will tolerate it and say no more on that subject. Your whore, bitch, slut on heat in Shelburne Bay – call her what you will – again, I am hurt by it but I will tolerate the pain it brings me. I shall say no more on it. But what I absolutely and flatly refuse to understand, to forgive, to tolerate, is what you did to Athenia."

"Oh dear God, no," and then he suddenly started weeping like a child chastised. "I have committed a great sin in a moment of weakness. God forgive me."

"He may forgive you but I never will and if I were you, I wouldn't go running to your woman in Shelburne Bay either. Alright, I said I wouldn't mention her any more but I was lying. You know about lying, don't you? She knows about all of what has been going on because I visited and confronted her about this business on the Friday just gone – two days before the wedding. I think she has a mind to cut your balls off if and when she sees you again.

"You are a philanderer, a drunkard and a base and wicked violator of innocence. Yes, I know what you did to Athenia, even though she was unconscious at the time and could not fend you off. I have seen the wickedness of lust in your eyes as she grew into a woman. I have seen that look of evil when you have lusted after her. You probably had that same look about you when you raped her. When you raped your own daughter who was betrothed to a young and innocent man. And whenever I look at you now, all I see is a godless, mean-spirited, vile and drunken son of a bitch!"

"That is enough!"

"No! No! No! It is not enough!" And she brought down the palm of her hand sharply on the table three times and sent the three quarters empty whiskey glass flying. It landed on the stone floor of the kitchen and shattered.

"It most certainly is not enough! I want you to leave my home now and never come back. You might as well take the car, which I paid for, because if it takes you as far away as it is possible to take you from this house and from me and from Athenia, then it has done a good job.

"If you make any effort to come back here or try to make contact with Athenia, I will call the chief of police and inform him that it was you who raped our daughter and that Frankie Miller is guilty only of what Athenia said he did. You swore an oath on the Holy Bible that it was Frankie Miller. You perjured yourself and your black soul will burn in hell for it. And you forced Athenia to commit that same act of perjury. You not only raped your own daughter, but on the witness stand, you made her commit the same perjorous act just to throw the scent off you. But how fortunate Judge Rheinhardt would only go for a charge of molesting. He couldn't try Frankie Miller for rape without a jury – and juries talk and trial by jury for rape generates publicity in the press.

"But I am just as responsible because I knew what was happening and thus, by remaining silent, I committed that same act of perjury. I perverted the course of justice, not only to protect the name and innocence of our daughter but to protect the good name and reputation of this family.

"Do you think I did it for you as well? No. If I could

have protected myself and Athenia in any other way, I would have had no compunction whatsoever in throwing you to the wolves and shaming you across the entire New England states."

"Pandora, don't do this. Can you not find it in your heart to forgive me my reckless and heinous sins? I'm sure the good Lord understands."

"You are beyond forgiveness, beyond redemption, and I'm sure the good Lord has already reserved a place for you in Hell.

"I may sell the house and the farm and move away. I'm undecided as yet. But I'm willing to bet the clucking hens of the congregation at church may sooner or later find out what really happened. I'm convinced of it. Will Frankie Miller tell his true story when he has served his time? If he had got the statutory ten to twenty years for rape, things would have been different. I would have owned up and allowed that pack of wolves to tear you to pieces.

"I'm not going to divorce you. Why should I offer you the comfort of a divorce when by not doing so you can never legally wed your lover in Shelburne Bay or anyone else for that matter while I live and breathe. At least not in this state you can't and assuming she is prepared to waste her life on a penniless wretch such as you. I am of course assuming she doesn't believe a damn word I told her. But I left her weeping bitter tears in her own front parlour on Friday.

"And she doesn't know about Frankie Miller either so don't you go telling her your lies. You know what I will do if you tell all. So don't bet on it, Ethan. You lose either way.

"No. No divorce. I want to make you suffer as much as I can. That is the only pleasure I shall have left in this life.

"Lucas Richmond was ten times the man you always were and my one regret in life is not defying my father's wishes when I had the opportunity to do so. How I always longed to have him inside of me, his arms around me." The mighty wall of her will collapsed for a brief second of time and her bottom lip quivered as she thought of Lucas. "But I got you instead. Daddy made me marry you, you slimy bastard."

She got another whiskey glass and filled it to the brim. She drank two thirds of it before she continued.

"I didn't for one moment believe you were man enough to ask my forgiveness but you did and I find it as insincere and as abhorrent as it could have been. You are as cowardly as any piece of dog shit in the gutter and I'm glad to be rid of you. See how long your slut in Shelburne Bay tolerates you because you won't get a cent from me. You came to me with nothing but your smart religious talk and I don't care how you leave. Just get out and stay out and I hope you rot in hell, you foul and disgusting mess of an alcoholic rake. Get out of my sight!" She threw the half empty glass of whiskey at him, but he ducked and it shattered against the stone wall of the kitchen.

He left. He said nothing, did nothing, except pack his personal belongings and walked out of the door.

Pandora never saw or heard of him again and neither did he ever see Athenia again.

****

On the afternoon of Monday March 6 1939, Ethan Saul turned up at his lover's home in Shelburne Bay and even before he had closed the gate to the garden at the front of her house, Frances Montpelier, thirty-six years of age and looking as beautiful as she did when she was half that age, appeared at the door of her home. She held a Winchester pump action shotgun in her hands and pointed it at Ethan Saul.

"The garden gate is far enough, Ethan. I don't want you in my home. Not now and not ever again."

"Let me explain, Frances."

"Explain what? You've been laying next to me for four years and I somehow guessed you had other women. They seem to be drawn to you like iron filings to a magnet. Mayhap you can explain those other women and I might find it in me to forgive you. But when your wife came to see me Friday just gone and told me you raped your own daughter, I went into my bathroom and threw up.

"So how in Christ Almighty's name can you now have the base gall to turn up on my doorstep and tell me you can explain? Can you truly explain how and why you raped your own daughter?"

"It was a moment of weakness. I couldn't stop myself."

"Couldn't stop yourself? Is that the very best you can do to atone for your sin? Ethan Saul, get off my property and get out of my sight before I blow your balls to kingdom come."

And she shucked a cartridge into the breech of the Winchester. He knew she would do it too.

Ethan dropped his head in resignation, turned and didn't even close the gate after him. He drove off in his car and Frances Montpelier never heard of or saw him again.

****

It soon became obvious to Ethan Saul that he hadn't a solitary friend in the State of Vermont so after a few days wandering around the state, he eventually motored down to his birthplace of Jackson, Tennessee. He wasn't known down here. It had been twenty-three years since he had last been here and he knew he would have little or no trouble in starting again.

What Pandora and no one else knew was that for his entire twenty three year tenure as the Pastor of Springwater Baptist Church, Ethan Saul had been skimming off the offertory collection boxes more or less on a weekly basis. The congregation of Springwater Baptist Church were always generous to a fault, even in hard times, but none of them suspected he had been taking up to twenty dollars a week from the box and stashing it away in a secret box hidden in the loft of the barn.

Thus, when Pandora told him to leave her house, he went straight to the loft of the barn and put his ill-gotten gains into his suitcase. He had amassed a little over twenty-two thousand dollars. At the very least, he would never starve in Jackson, Tennessee.

****

The population in Jackson was around twenty-four thousand and he guessed there were more than enough sinners here for him to start up another church. He rented a gone out of business garage in the back streets of the town centre, converted it into a church hall with a table for an altar, candlesticks of cheap brass and second hand benches he found at a rummage yard sale.

It was a start and with some luck (including a good deal of prayer – which he still firmly believed in) he just knew he would have the Church of the Redemption of Sinners up and running in no time at all.

For the first five years, things went well. There were plenty of sinners in this town for him to redeem but he himself was the worst of sinners in his congregation because he went back to his old habits of drinking strong whiskey and womanising.

Then things started to go wrong. Even after only five years, most of his money was gone on drink, womanising and fair weather friends (he had lost five thousand dollars as bribes to keep him away from the courts from two women chasing paternity suits) and at the end of six years, he hadn't two solitary cents to rub together (he remembered Pandora saying that to him just before she told him to leave her home).

His congregation had trickled down to virtually nothing and the courts were chasing money for unpaid rent on the land the church stood on. His congregation were a mixture of poor dirt farmers, those who were still out of work from the Great Depression and people who generally had no money at all so there had never been much money on the offertory plate for him to filch and hoard away. But what put the final nail in his coffin was the fact that he was riddled with syphilis and he was slowly losing his grip on life.

Broke and broken (even his thirteen year old car had given up on him) when no one turned up for the service on the morning of Sunday December 17 1944, Pastor Ethan Saul put a noose around his neck and hung himself. The last thought that went through his head was that this was the way his father had gone to meet his maker.

****

On Friday November 3 1939, Athenia Susanne de Francia gave birth to a daughter, Susanne-Marie and named her after her maternal grandmother. To all intents and purposes, the de Francia family were happy and settled in their home in Dorchester Hills, New Rochelle. Pandora had given the couple fifty per cent towards the cost of their new home, while Jorge Alejandro de Francia paid the other fifty per cent.

Remembering what her mother had said to her before her wedding – 'Knowledge is power' – Athenia, for six solid years, studied at her husband's *alma mater* for a degree in criminal law and on completion and with several years practice with a large New York Criminal Law firm, she set up the de Francia Criminal Law practice with sizeable funds given to her by her mother in exchange for a silent partnership.

By the time the Japanese had attacked Pearl Harbour, Pandora had sold Mockingbird Heights and its associated farm and forest land. The sprawling mansion was too big for one person (she would have no servants in the house) and the place was too full of bad memories for her to enjoy her twilight years. Even in summer now, it was cold and in the fall and winter, it was colder still and damp.

The property was sold to an Italian couple out of New York, he an East Side mobster and she his innocent wife. They lasted three years until rival gangsters from the New England Crime Syndicate, under instructions from New York, shot him to death as he lay in his bed.

The property was rented out to a few tenants over the next five years but none of them stayed for very long. They said the house was creepy, with a heavy atmosphere and some stated they had seen things which could not be rationally explained. What things, they never said.

And thus, from the beginning of the Korean War, the house became unoccupied on a permanent basis and like Poe's House of Usher, Mockingbird Heights languished into dust, mould and ignominious decay.

****

On selling Mockingbird Heights, Pandora Weston (she reverted to her maiden name because the name of Saul sickened her and she would have no more of him, not even in name) moved to Provincetown at the top of the promontory of Cape Cod. She bought an apartment in the town and settled into an uneasy life.

All of the time she had been married to Ethan Saul, she had been a committed Baptist but she now felt that God had interfered with her life once too often and now never went near any church. She lived her own life, minded her own business and never interfered with that of anyone else. She lived a solitary life and for all of her wealth, she remained, completely of her own free will, in almost total isolation.

It took six long years and numerous and (mainly) pointless visits to Alcoholics Anonymous and her psychiatrist's office in Boston before Pandora Weston was finally committed to an asylum, where she was soon diagnosed as being clinically insane, along with the onset of senile dementia.

Sometimes, she had drunk an entire bottle of whiskey a day and her doctors were astounded that she could go on drinking so much and not kill herself. But behind it all was Ethan. He had spent years drinking and womanising and (unknown to anyone, even Pandora) purloined money from his congregation when it should have gone to church funds. Perhaps, though, he was clever and astute and realised that one day his drinking and womanising habits would get him into serious trouble and he had to have something to fall back on. But the twenty-two thousand dollars he had amassed had all been but wasted. It gave him some brief years of pleasure but he was nevertheless destined to fall, and fall heavily. And Pandora suspected him of other wrongdoings as well: she didn't know what and neither did she want to know.

Ethan had lied to her over the years, consistently, cheated on her, soaked himself in whiskey and treated her like a low life dog. He had taken from her all the respect she had spent years building up and he had dishonoured her, destroyed every last ounce of trust she had in him by raping his own daughter and expecting forgiveness.

All of this played on her mind and there was nothing she did to check its progress. Over the next ten years, she gradually slipped and slid and tumbled into a nightmare world of alcoholism and deep depression which fed her insanity.

Pandora Weston passed on from this life on Tuesday April 4 1950 and very deep in her heart where no one could reach, Athenia breathed a sigh of relief on the death of her mother. But Athenia's one true and heartfelt wish was that her father was burning in Hell.

New Rochelle: 1954 – 1959

She had been in a hundred similar rooms of ten by eight where the walls were painted a dull cream or green or grey. Sometimes, it was white all over; a throwback from the Korean War when the intelligence services of both sides used pure white to send their most valued prisoners so psycho-crazy, they would talk when asked questions just so they could find peace in a darkened room.

The room was just an ordinary interview room inside the local precinct but it had seen child killers, kiddy molesters, rapists, armed robbers and mafia hoodlums by the score and everyone had left something behind them, an aura, an afterglow. She could smell them, smell their corruption and the nastiness of their crimes. It hung in the air like a cloying sickness and no matter how much the room was cleaned and disinfected, the disturbing atmosphere remained.

It didn't matter which precinct it was, she had always sensed the corruption within and spoken to some of those who had brought it with them. Had it been such experiences which had altered her own structure or had it been born within her? Beyond the fact of what she knew of her own father's vileness and her mother's decline into mental illness, she didn't know and neither did she care. Athenia de Francia was one of New York City's top criminal lawyers and the last thing on her mind on this day was the depth of her corruption, amoral or otherwise and how it came to be born.

As soon as she walked into the interview room at the precinct, she could smell the sleaze and dirt coming from him. It looked as if he hadn't shaved for a week and he smelled like he hadn't bathed or showered for longer. His clothes were scruffy and his shoes were scuffed, scratched and cracking from a lack of boot polish and general cleansing. He was an ex New York police detective by the name of Alessandro (Lucky) Lucania, who had been dismissed from the force on charges of corruption, organising sessions of child pornography and falsifying evidence – which was a real pity because he was a first class detective and under different circumstances, he could have climbed to higher heights. But he had fallen victim to the scent of bribe money and thus began his decline. The charges relating to child pornography had been dropped because the only witness had received a bullet in the head from a mob assassin outside Jack Dempsey's Broadway restaurant.

Lucania always swore, because of his surname, he was related to New York's Lucky Luciano, (Luciano's original name had been Lucania) the syndicate boss of bosses, and thus he earned the nickname of Lucky. Lucania now worked as a private detective and mainly on divorce cases where he photographed the cheating lovers in compromising positions.

Athenia de Francia's opinion of him as she walked into the room was 'obnoxious piece of shit' and she visibly turned her nose up at the unclean smell of rancid body odour and stale tobacco coming from him. Lucania now bragged that he worked for the mob because they sent an assassin to murder an only prosecution witness against him. Athenia figured this was far from the truth: she thought the mob had murdered the witness as a warning to Lucania because he knew far more than the pornography racket. But they left him alone because he was useful to them.

Here before her was a scared kitty cat who was on the verge of tears because standing before him was one of New York's most powerful criminal prosecution lawyers.

"Isn't it customary for a gentleman to stand when a lady walks into the room?" she said. "Though in your case, I use the word 'gentleman' with extreme caution."

He half rose from his chair.

"Don't bother, Mr. Lucania. If you have to be told to do something, it isn't worth the effort of doing.

"Let me lay a few facts on the line for you and that will help explain why I have appointed myself as your attorney. You are lucky in that respect because normally I deal only with prosecutions.

"I see you have been up to your old tricks again – amongst other things, hoarding child pornography for a so-called friend."

He smirked and said, "Yeah, but I'm -"

"Do not make the mistake of smirking at me. You're not as innocent as you make yourself out to be. In fact, give me three minutes in the witness box with you and I'll break you into a hundred pieces and you will get ten to twenty no problem.. Are you guilty of the charges or not? The truth now because otherwise, the deal I have for you is off."

"Yeah, okay. But I really was only looking after it for a friend."

"That's bullshit. And the deal is off if you keep lying to me. I'm going to have all of this pornographic material confiscated and burned in the incinerator where they dispose of drugs and illegal tobacco and other fire consumable goods. Meanwhile, all the charges against you are dropped and when I have finished with you today, you are free to go."

"So what's this deal? Promise to be a good boy in future?"

"I forgot to mention, no sarcasm either or the deal is off. If you agree to the deal, well, we have a deal. If you don't agree to it, I'll lay charges on you which you wouldn't even begin to believe and you'll be in a cell in Sing Sing before your nasty stinky little feet touch the ground.

"Other prisoners, particularly lifers and those on

death row, don't like child pornographers."

"I told you, I'm innocent. I was just hoarding the stuff for a friend and I never looked at it so I didn't know what it was. He was the guy..."

"Shushushushush! Do not say another word in your defence. Do you have any idea what they do to kiddy fiddlers in prison?"

"Hey! Come on! What's with the kiddy fiddling? I never touched no kids. I swear on my mother's grave. You try and lay those charges on me and I'll -"

"And you will what, Mr. Lucania? I can lay these charges on you, fake the evidence and make the charges stick like shit to a blanket. So don't you have the audacity to threaten me.

"Now then, here is the deal. You were holding the photographs for a friend, one Johnny Disano, a fifth rate mobster who is known to you but has now disappeared. What do you think, Mr. Lucania?"

"I swear he gave me a sealed envelope to keep for him. I didn't know what was inside. He paid me five hundred bucks to look after it for him."

"Until you looked."

"Until I looked. Hey, come on. I was curious. He was into smuggling Mexicans across the border into Texas and New Mexico, California, wherever, so I thought it might be something like forged passports or visas. I thought it might be hot money or forged notes. But I never thought for one moment it was those photographs."

"Curious? Ye gods, I've never seen anything so disgusting in all of my life. I never once realised that men in this day and age could sink so low."

"What do I say to him when he comes back for the

goods? If I don't have the goods, he'll break my legs – and take back his money!"

"I don't think you need to worry about Mr. Disano. Truly, no one knows where he is. My bet is he'll turn up somewhere like the bottom of the East River wearing a pair of concrete slippers. Either that or some waste site out in the sticks. Appropriate place for him, don't you think?

"Now, you deny ever opening the envelope. The envelope was sealed and you're not the nosey type. Do you understand me so far?"

"Yeah."

"The answer should be 'Yes, Mrs. De Francia, I fully understand.' Don't 'yeah' me please. It shows such a lack of respect." And she raised her left eyebrow at him.

He caught her drift very quickly and said, "Yes, Mrs. De Francia, I understand."

"Then we understand each other. In return for getting you off these charges, I want your services. Because you are nosey, you have a penchant for gathering information. I have a list of names and addresses I shall give you. They are some of my friends and neighbours in Dorchester Hills, New Rochelle County and quite naturally in general conversation, they are not forthcoming with the information I want on them.

"This is where you come in. I want everything on them. Where their kids go to school. Are these kids in trouble with the law? Is mom or dad having an affair? What are mom and dad's habits they would rather not make known to their friends and neighbours? What are they involved with? Who are they involved with? Do any of them have criminal records?

"I'll pay you a retainer fee of five hundred dollars a month, to be paid on the last business day of the month I nominate and in cash and you can collect it from me personally at my office between the hours of nine and ten.

"Do not let me down on this because if you screw up on this deal, I'll make sure I'm not around to help you out of the mire."

"You can count on me, Mrs. De Francia."

"I know I can. Here is an envelope which contains the names and addresses I want investigating and a two hundred and fifty dollar bonus for taking on the deal.

"A few final points, Mr. Lucania. This deal is very strictly between the two of us and you will not discuss this with anyone else, even your closest confidante. Not your girlfriends, not your dime whores, not your detective friends, not even the guy who picks up the dog shit from the street. Remember what I said about being able to make trumped up charges stick.

"Here is my card with a direct line to me. If you want to speak to me and I'm in my office, I'll speak to you. Also, if you want to see me, you do so at my office. Don't you dare ever turn up at my home. If you want to see me at a time other than that which we have arranged, you telephone me and give me twenty-four hours notice.

"I want your first report on the day you pick up your first five hundred dollars and that is six weeks away – let me see, report back to me on Friday April 30. Now you can go. And for Christ's sake, take a bath. You stink like a Bowery hobo.

"By the way, if you get caught, you will not mention my name or identify me by any other means. If you do, be assured of two things. One, I will vehemently deny that I told you to do certain things and two, I will bring these child pornography charges back against you. You will notice the negatives are missing. I have them safely deposited and they act as my insurance against you in case you try to double-cross me.

"I would never try to..."

"I know you won't. I know that for a fact."

"And don't try to cheat me on the information you give me. I can get people to double check what you tell me and if I find you have lied to me, mayhap I'll get the mob to but a bullet in your kneecaps as a short sharp lesson. I do have connections you know.

"And finally, if you do take photographs – and my information tells me that you can – I will take possession of all pictures and negatives. If you try to use any for your own means, well, don't even think about it because as soon as I suspect you are doing it, I will bring charges against you that will stick.

"Now you can go and I strongly suggest you use some of that two hundred and fifty dollar bonus to kit yourself out with some new clothes. Don't ever again come into my office or presence like you are now."

****

What goes on behind closed doors and in the very strict privacy of one's home is nobody's business but the owner of the house or apartment. If whoever is doing whatever and it does not break any state or federal law, then outsiders may not be permitted to know what goes on behind those closed doors. To some of them, what they do may be hugely embarrassing if it might be made public and in these times of taboo-ridden middle and upper class America, they dare not be found out.

Homosexuals, cross dressers, members of the Communist Party, racketeers, national and local politicians involved in seedy behaviour and corruption of a sexual or financial nature: many had gone to ground and were hiding themselves well. But some ran from cover and were leaving themselves wide open to federal investigation or blackmail.

One would think that behind the closed doors of these hugely expensive homes and apartments in upper class New Rochelle, normal life prevailed but the Kinsey Reports of the late 1940's and early 1950's painted a very different picture and even Kinsey and his associates failed to report on the most secret of secrets.

****

When night falls and most people sleep, there may be things going on which many of us would rather not know about. Apart from criminal activity (which, at night or in the early hours of the morning, is expected) we pretend that all is well with the world and our neighbourhood and thus, we sleep soundly.

Henry Flemyng had never married and inherited his wealth from his doting parents, who had been twenty years in their graves. He was their only child. He was pleasant enough and possessed the social skills necessary for a comfortable life in New Rochelle. He was a wealthy man who had his own coin dealership in Manhattan in an office block on Fifth Avenue. His specialty was gold coins from the 17th to the 19th centuries, with a further specialty in rare Middle East coinage. His bread and butter business was trading Krugerands and English sovereigns and half sovereigns. All was at peace in his world and he kept his secret well hidden.

But Alessandro Lucania always thought that if a guy was unmarried and in his early forties (and was as good looking and as slim as Flemyng was) he must have something to hide and thus, one morning, he watched Henry Flemyng leave for his coin dealership in Manhattan, waited twenty minutes and then broke into his house to see what he could find. It was pitifully easy with the set of keys he had.

He emerged two hours later not disappointed, a cool smirk on his face and leaving everything as he had found it, except for some photographs and negatives.

Flemyng returned at three in the afternoon (Lucania had been watching him on a regular basis so he had some idea of his habits – but today was Wednesday and he always had a half day on Wednesdays) ate a light meal, showered and then began the ritual of his transformation from man to woman.

Flemyng was slim and looked younger than his forty-two years and the shape of his face was somewhat removed from being manly. There was very little beard growth and his complexion was midway between dark and pale. He spent a full hour applying mascara, a little rouge, eye makeup, eyelashes, lipstick and a wig of brunette curls. Then he applied painted false nails. He half filled two breast-shaped latex rubber containers with warm water, sealed each of them with a small tightly fitting stopper and inserted them into the black brassiere he had put on, followed by panties, garter belt and nylon stockings and then a black, ankle length evening gown with black patent leather medium heeled shoes.

He left his home in the early evening when it was dark (he thought no one could recognise him in the dark and the one time somebody mentioned they had seen a woman coming out of his house at night, he said it was his cousin from Yonkers – and once, while he was getting ready, someone came knocking at his door and he couldn't leave his home until he was sure they had gone) and Lucania followed him in his car.

Lucania followed him all the way into Greenwich Village to a very private club (members only) on Seventh Avenue. He photographed him going in, while he was in the club (he still had his police identification and it could get him into places to which he normally would not be able to gain entry - who was going to complain?) and leaving the club with a girlfriend (boyfriend?). He followed them to an address in Queens, took a few more photographs and then went home to develop them. Looking at the developed photographs, yes the other person was a guy and not as clever as Flemyng in applying a woman's makeup.

He dealt with David de Kuyper in much the same way, noting the pattern of him leaving his home and the times he returned on certain days. Lucania broke into de Kuyper's home at just past one on a Friday morning when he knew de Kuyper would be spending the night elsewhere; exactly where, he didn't know but he would find out next time because then he would follow him.

He had to pick the lock on a hidden cabinet drawer (must have something to hide, Lucania thought) to get to what he wanted. He found a manila sized brown envelope containing photographs of de Kuyper and his boyfriend in some extremely compromising positions and in various states of undress. De Kuyper was around sixty years of age and the young man in the picture was, by Lucania's estimate, not above twenty-five. He looked through three more envelopes he found in the drawer but didn't find any photographs involving minors (he was a little disappointed at that) and most of the photographs (some in colour but most in black and white) were of the same young man and Lucania figured this is whom he might bed with when staying on a Thursday evening.

He took half a dozen of the photographs, each from different envelopes, to use as evidence (who was going to prove he took them if Mrs. De Francia wanted them only for her own perusal?). He also took the negatives of the same photographs.

He waited until the following Thursday morning to

follow him to his place of work, a major banking corporation in Manhattan's South Houston District, waited until four in the afternoon until he came out of his office and followed him to an address in Brooklyn and then to a gay club in one of Brooklyn's back streets. He took photographs of the two leaving the apartment in Brooklyn and some of them entering a Brooklyn gay club.

He followed the same procedure with Wilma Vernon, who occasionally went to dining clubs, the movies or to the occasional bar with a female friend but he could prove nothing untoward in that. What he could prove, however, was that Wilma Vernon was a fully paid up member of the Communist Party USA. He took photographs of all of the documents involved and left the house. He was lucky: Wilma Vernon returned to her home (unplanned) two minutes after he left. Close shaves he did not like.

Lucania still retained a couple of friends on the police force, both corrupt detectives: they were the ones who had not been caught and of whom Lucania knew a considerable amount more than the Captain of the precinct. Thus, for a nominal sum, they were more than prepared to offer him the occasional favour when he wanted the lowdown on someone or when he wanted some money because he was broke.

Lucania gave a name to one of the detectives and asked him if she was a known name (someone who might be under investigation for whatever reason). The result came back as positive. Laura Benito was currently under silent investigation on suspicion of running a high class call girl racket. She had a son, Roberto, and her husband. Christiano Benito, was a jeweller to high society and also a serial womaniser. There were only suspicions because she was too clever and like mafia bosses, she had created buffer zones between herself and those who worked for her. She occasionally turned a trick herself, but only for a very few favoured clients – and she was *very* expensive. This was her only mistake and Lucania picked up on it.

He picked up on the fact that every Tuesday morning at ten thirty precisely, she left her home in New Rochelle's northern district and drove to a motel some twenty miles north east. She remained at the motel until middle to late afternoon and then returned home.

The owner of the motel allowed Lucania to see the register because Lucania threatened him with exposure to the local police for hiring out rooms for immoral purposes. His police identification was like an ingot of solid gold in circumstances such as these.

Lucania had thought it pathetic that she had spent the afternoon with Mr. John Smythe (oh please, he thought, let's have some originality here!) in Room Number 44 and the fact that the room number was the same every week. He thought maybe he could rent the room next door and install a movie camera – but he decided to sit on this one for another time.

He followed her to this very same room over the next three weeks, took photographs and copies of the motel register. Lucania was beginning to appreciate this kind of work.

All of these people Athenia knew extremely well and encompassed them in her circle of close friends. They all had their secrets; nasty, tasteless, embarrassing or otherwise, but Athenia now knew their secrets and stored them for possible future use.

****

"Well, Mrs. De Francia," Alessandro Lucania said, "this envelope contains a number of photographs, negatives and my written report. I have to warn you, however, that some of the photographs are not very pleasant. Also, the most unpleasant ones are from private collections and removed from the homes without knowledge or permission of the owners. I don't know how you can get round that in a court of law."

"Who said anything about taking these and the owners to court? Knowledge is power, Mr. Lucania. What about the negatives?"

"There are no negatives for the photographs I removed from private property and maybe the negatives are held in a safe but I'm no safecracker. But in essence, I don't believe there are any negatives because I found all of the photographs in locked drawers or cabinets which are fairly easy to pick if you have the right keys. And I do. If they thought the photographs were safe in locked drawers and cabinets, why didn't they keep the negatives with the photographs? No, I don't believe the negatives exist any more. However, the photographs I took myself, all the negatives are there."

He had kept the negatives he had stolen and thought he might make some blackmail money on them at some time in the future, contrary to Athenia's wishes and fully aware of what might happen if he was caught. But he was prepared to take the gamble.

"And copies?"

"There are no copies."

"Are you sure of that?"

"You are going to have to trust me on that one, Mrs. De Francia, but I recall every word of our previous conversation and I have taken note. I'm not into blackmail and in that envelope are all of the photographs and necessary negatives."

She looked briefly at each of the black and white photographs. "My, my, Mr. Lucania, you certainly have been a busy bee. I think it is safe to assume you have earned your money this month." She handed him an envelope. "There is your five hundred for this month and next month, I'll include an extra two hundred and fifty for these privately acquired photographs. One more question. Are any of these photographs doctored in any way?"

"Not a one of them. It's all genuine stuff."

"So if necessary, they will stand up in court?"

"All of those photographs are genuine. As genuine as the Mona Lisa in the Louvray (his French pronunciation was at garbage level). You can have them looked over by a professional photographer if you want, but he will tell you the same. They are all one hundred per cent genuine."

"I'll take your word for it. You have information on the most important names on the list I gave you. And Wilma Vernon! Now there's a surprise I didn't expect. The remainder I'm in no hurry for and what you might find may not even be worth my effort but I'll pay you a retainer for the next three months anyway. Put these dates in your diary: Monday, May 31; Wednesday, June 30 and Friday, July 30. Those are the dates I want to see you here in my office with any further information you may have gleaned. And don't forget, between the hours of 9 and 10.

"The next job, however, is a little more difficult." She gave him a slip of paper with a name, a place of birth and a date of birth. "This man is – was – my father; Ethan Saul, a minister of the Baptist Church. His last known address was Mockingbird Heights in Rutland, Vermont, but you won't find any information there. I suggest you begin your search in Jackson, Tennessee where he was born and which is where I suspect he might have returned after he left Vermont. But other than that, I have no further information. I'll take that information from you when you come and see me May 31. Discretion at all times, Mr. Lucania. Discretion.

If he is still alive and you find him, you will not mention my name. If he is dead, so be it but you will still not mention my name to anyone. Until next time, Mr. Lucania, goodbye."

****

Liking someone and loving them are two completely different ends of a spectrum and thus, Athenia liked Tomas but she had precious little love for him. Her mother had seen the marriage as a business deal and love never entered the arrangement. But Athenia always put on a good show of being the loving wife in New Rochelle society. She didn't hate Tomas, but at the same time, she didn't love him.

Soon after their marriage and when she told Tomas she was pregnant, they moved to the Dorchester Hills neighbourhood of New Rochelle in South Westchester, New York State so that Tomas could comfortably study for his finals at law school and Athenia could enrol at the same school. The administrators frowned (but very kindly) at the fact that she was 'with child' (as one kindly senior lady put it) but they hadn't bargained on her determination to succeed. She refused any bursary or financial assistance because she had the money from her mother (an advance on her inheritance) to fund her education at the university.

She knew she would succeed because she had always had a strong penchant for criminal law (encouraged by her sudden interest before her marriage into the legal aspects of incestuous rape) and this was confirmed when six years after enrolling, she graduated valedictorian in her subject of Criminal Law in New York State.

By the beginning of the 1950's decade, the de Francia Criminal Law practice, though rather small in scale when compared to others, was astoundingly influential and its head, Athenia de Francia, felt it was what she deserved after what she had gone through prior to her marriage. She hadn't heard of or from her father since the day of her marriage and thus, she was hoping for some solid information from Alessandro Lucania on his next scheduled meeting with her.

When he returned some weeks later on the appointed date, he had all of the information she required. She thanked him profusely and added a several hundred dollars bonus to his payment.

She took time out of her schedule and over a few days, drove a thousand miles to Jackson, Tennessee and then to Ridgeacre Cemetery on Ridgeacre Road, located Ethan Saul's final resting place and poured a large soda bottle of her urine over it. Then she spat on his grave until she could spit no more. She was pleased that finally, she had been able to carry out her threat that she would piss and spit on his grave if she ever found it.

She booked into a local motel for that night and drove back home to New York State over the next three days.

It was a long way to travel both ways just so she could do what she had done, but the compulsion to do it was years old and it had never died within her, but now, she could have final closure on that part of her life.

In the years since she had left home, she had become very powerful and very rich in her pursuit of wealth and knowledge in her profession and inheriting her mother's wealth on her death was an added bonus. She had also inherited her mother's quiet but solid determination that what she wanted, she would eventually have and for the most part, she had succeeded.

****

Anybody who was anybody in New Rochelle society was at the de Francia garden party on Saturday November 4 1954 to help celebrate the fifteenth birthday of their daughter, Susanne-Marie. There was at least two Senators and one Congressman, a few judges, attorneys (but only those who were listed as being part of Athenia's exclusive circle of friends), other political notables, personally invited neighbours, sundry acquaintances – and there was also room for a dozen of Susanne-Marie's school friends, of whom Roberto Benito (only son of Laura and Christiano Benito) was one and since he was the only boy she had invited (because he was the sole object of her girlish fantasies – of which content she never told her mother – and he was nearly two years her senior) she had her eyes set carefully on him. Today, she was going to have some fun.

All were swanning around each other like flies to dog mess; all were vying for favoured positions with the host and hostess (she being of supreme importance, he simply the obedient lap dog). All wanted to share the fruitiest of gossip, whether it be truth, rumour or downright lies: it didn't matter, so long as it got them a valued position in the scheme of things for today.

But Athenia threw out a false sense of security for some of those buzzing around her because those who buzzed the most, she had information on them which they thought she or no one else knew anything about. But she knew that what she knew about them would socially destroy them, their families and their standing on various local committees, school governorships, arts foundations etcetera, etcetera, etcetera and she danced them at the end of her puppet strings.

It might only be her daughter's fifteenth birthday party, but Athenia had transformed it into a fully functioning social gathering and Susanne-Marie wished the only one of her friends she had invited had been Roberto (Robbie) Benito. The eleven others, well, she could do without their soppy, girlish squealing and teenage pretend swooning over Roberto Benito (they wanted to share him) and Dean Martin singing *That's Amore*. All of their eyes were on Roberto but Susanne-Marie gave each of them a warning flash of her Spanish blue eyes which told them to lay off because

Roberto was hers and hers alone. They encroached on her territory at their peril. This she had inherited from her mother and she could be just as determined.

****

At the age of fifteen, the level of her desire for subterfuge, strategy and plot was just as advanced as that of a mature adult and her sole desire was to get Roberto Benito alone in a room in the house just so she could see what he was made of. She wanted him badly but if he turned out to be a cry baby candy-ass sissy, she would send him packing and rethink her strategy.

****

Frank Sinatra was singing some Italian love song and Susanne-Marie and Roberto Benito were smooching away on the makeshift dance floor to the rhythm. She kept putting her arms tighter around his waist, leaning her head on his shoulder so she could whisper her dirty talk in his ear. And then it began to happen. She took her head away from his shoulder and stared him in the eyes.

"Robbie!" she said. "If you want to get roused and excited, do not make it so obvious."

"I can't help it. You keep snuggling up to me saying things to me and I can't help the way I feel."

And she whispered in his ear, "Do you want me to put my hand down the front of your pants and see to that growing bulge? I saw you giving me the eye in church last Sunday morning and yesterday at school. We can go somewhere in the house."

"I don't know. I don't want your parents exploding if they discover us."

"Won't happen. My dad never watches me. It's my mom we have to be careful of. She has eyes like a hawk and sometimes, I think she watches my every move."

"What are we going to do then?"

"I'll go into the house and take a couple of friends with me. I'll send them packing ten minutes later and that is the signal for you to come up to my room. Turn right at the top of the stairs and it's the second on the left. And don't back out. I'll have a surprise waiting for you."

Robbie started to sweat in anticipation. He left the dancefloor and waited on the side, watched her disappear with two of her girlfriends and couldn't believe his incredible luck. He could hardly wait until he saw the guys again on Monday and mayhap he wouldn't say a thing; perhaps just wait until they were simply seen together and watch their jaws drop and their countenances turn green with sheer envy.

He wandered around for a few minutes, moved closer to the kitchen entrance to the house, but most of all, he kept an eye on Athenia (yakkety-yakking to her very select clique of hangers-on) but she was too busy with them to notice his movement towards the house and it didn't look like she had any eye looking out for Susanne-Marie.

Susanne-Marie's two friends appeared shortly after he sat down at the kitchen table and as they moved out into the garden, he looked for Athenia one last time and saw she was moving further away down the crowded garden to chat with more of her friends. Robbie disappeared up the stairs, turned right at the top and stood outside the second door on the left.

He knocked and said, "Susie? Are you in there? Can I come in?"

"You can come in. Robbie."

Robbie walked in and Susanne-Marie was standing with her back to her bedroom window and her cotton blouse fastened only by the bottom three buttons; the rest left nothing to Robbie's imagination and she was not wearing a brassiere.

"You forgot to close the door, Robbie. We wouldn't want anyone walking in on us, would we?"

"No, I guess we...er...we wouldn't. What am I supposed to do?"

"You mean you don't know? Don't you know anything about girls?"

"Yes...er...no...I mean..."

"We know an awful lot about boys. *I* know an awful lot about boys and what they want. And part of what they want is this."

Robbie gasped and stood there rooted to the spot with his mouth wide open as she undid the remaining buttons and dropped her cotton blouse to the floor, exposing her naturally large breasts to him. She lifted them in her hands and said, "Come on, Robbie, touch them and see what they feel like."

He moved forward a few steps and outstretched his hands. She took them and placed them on her flesh, moved his hands around.

He began to get too eager, getting the wrong message from her, but he wasn't thinking straight. He began to loosen the belt on his pants and Susanne-Marie stepped back.

"Oh no, Robbie Benito. You are going to have to wait for the real prize – I'm not even sixteen yet. How long can you wait, Robbie?"

"I know girls at school who do it all the time," he said.

"Well I'm not other girls, Robbie. I am me. And if you think for one moment I'm going to let you have your wicked way with me, I have a big disappointment for you that is as big as that bulge in your jockeys. You're not shoving that inside of me. I'm waiting for the right guy to happen along."

"Oh but aren't you so very adult. You invited me up here so what else did you expect? What was I supposed to think? What was I supposed to do?"

"Just fool around is all. Can't you get by with just a little fooling around? Supposing I was to get pregnant? Do you use protection?"

"Protection? What's that?"

She raised her eyes to the heavens, picked up her blouse and put it back on, along with her brassiere (she did not want her mother telling her to do this for the sake of decency). "Forget it, Robbie. How do you expect girls to treat you with respect if you don't know the first thing to do? When I said protection, I meant condoms."

"Oh those!"

"Yes, oh those. Have you any on you now?"

"No, I –"

"Then we'll go back to the party and have a boring time. You know, tedious people to thank for tedious birthday gifts, tedious adults to try and be 'adult' with. Whereas all I want is a good time in the privacy of my own room and you haven't even got any protection with you?"

She walked out of her room and he followed. "Fucking cock teaser, "he muttered.

Susanne-Marie returned to the party and mingled with her parents, their adult friends and one by one, dismissed her school friends. Robbie was the last.

"I heard what you said when we were leaving my room. If that is what you think I am, we can finish our relationship now. If you want to wait until you can be a smidge more adult about this, then we can discuss it at school on Monday. But if I were you, I would pay far more attention in biology class and read up on the subject. And don't you dare ever see me as an easy lay again."

He was right, she thought, as she lay in bed that night. I am a cock teaser and I do it because I like to do it. It gives me a sense of fun, of power. I want my men friends to be humbled before me and then I can have me some real fun!

****

But Susanne-Marie didn't have as easy a time as she thought she would. She chased Robbie Benito for almost a year but he decided he was going to play hard to get, just to teach her a lesson, that she couldn't have everything she wanted just by the click of her fingers. And mayhap he *had* paid attention in biology classes and discovered what a heap of trouble he could get himself (and a young lady) into if he started fooling around with the female of the species without paying too much attention to detail and how he should go about it. And the more she chased after him, the more fixated with him she became. Even the hunk who was the captain of the school baseball team didn't come up to scratch as far as she was concerned. For the foreseeable future, it was Robbie or no one.

But she knew all along, even through the dark days of the fall and winter and the months of the new year when all seemed lost, she knew that persistence would pay off. And Robbie fell like a brick in water and it was as if there had been no in between from her fifteenth birthday party to now, late in September of the following year.

****

On the last Thursday of the month, Susanne-Marie feigned illness and thus Athenia telephoned the school secretary and gave a seemingly valid explanation for her absence. Robbie sneaked a day off school and called at Susanne-Marie's house after he saw her mother drive off for her office. He even parked his car (his mother's car) in their driveway as brash as brash could be.

They watched a soppy romantic movie on TV, kissed and cuddled and then Susanne-Marie said she wanted to step things up a notch or two and thus led Robbie by the hand to her bedroom.

"Susie, I don't want to get us both into trouble."

"Don't be a bore, Robbie. I have no intention of going the whole way. But there are other ways we can have fun. Let me show you how. Come on now, don't be shy. Oh, by the way, I've left my pocketbook downstairs. Would you fetch it for me please? It's on the coffee table in front of the TV."

He obeyed like a lapdog and when he returned, Susanne-Marie was standing facing the mirror on her dresser and wore only a black negligee type of garment. She turned to Robbie and let the garment slip from her.

"Hello, Robbie," she said and smiled her wicked spider's smile.

Robbie's eyes widened out of all proportion as he watched, as if in slow motion, the black peignoir slip over her shoulders to land in a heap at her feet.

She stood before him as naked as the day she was born, her hands on her hips and she said, "Well, Robbie, are you going to stand there goggle-eyed all day or are you going to teach this very bad girl what she should do with a beautiful hunk such as you? Come on, Robbie. You know this is what you have been waiting for. No straight sex but let's just fool around for a while. We can have us some real fun."

"What…what do I do? I mean -"

"You mean to tell me you have never seen a girl naked before? Robbie, have you ever had a date?"

"Er...yes, sort of...I...er..."

"Oh my God but you're a cherry blossom! I don't believe it!"

"Hey, I've been with girls before."

"But you ain't never seen one butt naked."

"No...but –"

"Never mind. This is my first time too. Don't you think I'm bold and brash?"

He started to say something but she put her index finger on his lips to silence him. This was not the time for talk – or confessions.

They embraced in a long kiss and she unbuckled his belt and let his pants drop to the floor. This was his signal to take the rest off.

She gently prised his jaw apart and inserted her tongue into his mouth and it slopped around inside while little groans came from the back of his throat. He felt the soft puppy fat flesh of her buttocks and forced her closer to him. She felt his stiffness touch her stomach and she swayed slowly from left to right, exciting him and forcing his breath to come in shorter gasps and the moans from his throat to increase slightly in crescendo.

Susanne-Marie withdrew her tongue and licked his throat all over, then moved her lips along his chest, down to his stomach and finally dropped to her knees. She didn't ask him what he wanted her to do next and he was too far away in the land of ecstasy to care. She went straight for the kill and took his erection in between the thumb and index finger of her hand and kissed it and held it to her cheeks and played her lips along its entire length. She touched it with her tongue and heard him draw in his breath as wave after wave of ecstasy shot through him – and then she closed her lips around it at the tip and slowly allowed it to sink inside.

Since Susanne-Marie's bedroom was at the rear of the house, they didn't hear Athenia's car come along the driveway. But then it was only two in the afternoon and she was not expected home for another four hours

Athenia had had a hectic morning in her office and she didn't want another like it. Her 'business at the office' headache, compounded with a sniffle or three, was pounding, her throat was painfully dry and thus, since she was the boss, she decided on taking the rest of the day off and drove back to New Rochelle. She intended to shower, dose up with Tylenol and then take a long nap in bed.

She didn't recognise the car on the drive (in her parking space!) and wondered to whom it belonged.

She went in through the front door and going up the stairway, she heard girlish giggling noises coming from Susanne-Marie's bedroom – and a male voice.

She looked through the crack between the door and door post and saw them and what they were doing. She moved away from the door to her own study and returned with a thin bamboo cane in her hand.

The bedroom door opened quietly and slowly and the next thing Robbie knew was a sharp crack and instantaneous pain on his butt. He yelped in pain and drew back several feet as Athenia laid a single stroke of a bamboo cane across his butt.

"Just what the hell is going on here? " she said.

Susanne-Marie grabbed her peignoir and covered her nakedness as she said, "Oh my God, mother!"

"And you, young man, get yourself dressed in thirty

seconds or I will drag you out on to the street as you are."

"Mother, we were only fooling around."

"Not one more word, Susanne-Marie. I will deal with you soon enough."

Athenia grabbed Robbie by the scruff of his neck and dragged him out of the room, down the stairway and to the main entrance of the house.

He turned to face her. "Mrs. De Francia - " he began to say in apology but she struck him with her clenched fist and sent him flying through the open door into the porch area. She bloodied his nose and top lip.

She snatched at his ear and dragged him to his car. "For future reference, young man, this is my parking space. How old are you, Robbie?"

"I'm almost eighteen, Mrs. De Francia. Listen, it wasn't like it seemed."

"Almost eighteen? What it seemed like to me was my daughter is just short of her sixteenth birthday and the two of you were on the verge of having sex or whatever filthy and degenerate perversion you were indulging in. I know who you are. You are Laura Benito's son. Now you get the hell off my property and if I ever even catch you within one hundred yards of my home again I'll horsewhip you until you curse your mother for giving birth to you – do I make myself very clearly understood? Don't bother to answer. Just make yourself very scarce."

She returned to Susanne-Marie's bedroom. "And just what do you think you were doing with that young man?"

"We were not going the whole way. We were just fooling around."

"Fooling around? Well, let me tell it the way I saw it – and don't bother to dress. Firstly, you lied to me this morning when you said you were too ill to go to school. I will not be lied to, especially when there is base deceit involved.

"But fooling around? Is that what you call what you were doing? You were kneeling before him and doing – well, I can't even bring myself to say the word, filthy and degenerate practice that it is and I really cannot imagine where you learned that from. Not only will I have to make a serious attempt at controlling your behaviour in future but also your reading material, which I hardly think you got in the school library or learned in biology class."

She took Susanne-Marie by the upper arm and dragged her out of her room and into her own study at the end of the landing. She held her over her desk and said, "I will thrash this filthy and disgusting behaviour out of you. It is an abomination of the procreative act and I will have no bastard child in this house."

And then she began to lay the cane across her but Susanne-Marie refused to cry out. It hurt her physically but she refused to give her mother the satisfaction of crying out for her to stop.

She would remember this act of chastisement for the rest of her days; not as an act of punishment but as a coming of age, an enlightening experience. She enjoyed it to the pinnacle of her ecstasy and thought: de Sade never even dreamed of such an experience!

****

Tomas returned home later that evening and after greeting his daughter in her room, he went downstairs and confronted Athenia. She told him how she had discovered Susanne-Marie and her boyfriend and that she had feigned illness to take the day off school.

"I did what I felt it was necessary to do and that is an

end to the matter."

"But you beat her to within an inch of her life!"

"Don't exaggerate. I thrashed her with a cane is all. The matter is closed and I will not discuss it with you any further. You can go and tell her to come down for the evening meal."

Tomas knew better than to argue the point; Athenia had total control over him and in their house, like her office, her word was law.

Susanne-Marie sat at the table, her eyes looking downward and not daring to speak.

Athenia said, "Before you begin to eat, I believe an apology for your disgraceful behaviour is in order."

"Athenia," Tomas said. "This really is not the time and place to discuss the matter. Can we not allow things to settle and discuss it tomorrow?"

"Keep out of this, Tomas. I have already made my position on this matter very crystal clear to you. I will not have my home turned into a place where my fifteen year old daughter feels she is free to skip a day at school in order to indulge in the kind of degenerate practices I saw her engaged in and as if it is nothing more than a cheap thrill game – and certainly not before she takes her marriage vows!"

"But we were not going all the way, mother."

"Don't you dare speak out of turn again! Do so again and you will leave this table to go to your room and there you will stay until I decide you are fit to leave it.

"I will find it difficult to trust you again and you certainly will not be allowed boyfriends in the house again unless it is under my personal and strictest supervision. Didn't you even consider using protection? It doesn't look as if he even had the brains to think of that. Did penetration take place? And remember if I once believe you are lying to me, I will have you examined by a doctor, you shameless and depraved little slut."

"No, mother. I swear things never got that far and I never intended to go that far."

"Until further notice, when you return from school, you will go to your room and engage in your studies. You will also do this at weekends and this will remain in force until I decide you have learned your lesson.

In bed that night, Susanne-Marie listened to a heated discussion between her mother and father. During the argument, Tomas mentioned that she has been seen in her office with a seedy private detective.

"True, but I do not see why I should have to explain myself to you because someone at the office tattle-tales about who I am seen with and who I permit into the confines of my own office. Anyway, it is perfectly – well, almost – innocent."

"Innocent? Getting this guy to snoop on your society friends so you can dish the dirt on them?"

"Thank you, Tomas. I will find out who gave you the information and they will lose their job for it. But knowledge is power, Tomas. My mother taught me that. Knowledge is power."

There was a telephone call later that evening from Laura Benito and she demanded to see Athenia the very next day regarding a serious assault on her son. Athenia agreed to a mid-day meeting, only because she had been caught in the right mood and she was just itching for a showdown. This is where information she had gained from Alessandro Lucania was going to come in useful and pay many dividends.

****

The following day at precisely the appointed time, Laura Benito drew up in her car on the driveway of the de Francia household. Athenia was waiting for her and she approached the car as it pulled up in the driveway (actually, it skidded to a halt because Laura Benito was in the foulest of moods and was just itching for a fight).

"Don't bother to get out of the car, Laura. I don't want you in my home."

"Well that suits me fine but I have to tell you I'm here because my son has complained that you assaulted him several times yesterday and one of those assaults involved him being whipped with a bamboo cane. And you also broke his nose, goddamnit! I'll have you in court for this."

"Don't threaten me with court action, Laura. At least not until you have the full facts. And these are the facts.

"Do you know what I caught your son doing yesterday – and in my home?. By the way, did you know he wagged off school yesterday? Or were you too busy with Mr. John Smythe to even care about what your son was getting up to?"

"Mister who?"

"Oh, excuse me but that is Tuesday, isn't it?"

"What are you talking about?"

"Never mind that. You were talking about seeing me in court?"

"Yes and besides the bamboo cane, you dragged him by his hair through your house and punched him in the face before you physically threw him out of your house."

"Yes, I admit to all of that but I did not break his nose. I bloodied it and also his top lip. He got what he asked for."

"What? You goddamn brazen bitch!"

"Before we revert to name calling, Laura, I think you ought to listen to me and I will give you the full facts."

"They had better stand up because I'm on the verge of calling in the police and what will that do to your professional career?"

"It will do nothing detrimental because the police are not going to be involved and neither shall you see me in court so my professional career remains intact. But the facts, Laura. Listen to the facts.

"Yes, I fully and openly admit assault. Why did I assault your son with a bamboo cane? Why did I drag him through my home by his hair? Why did I sock him in the mouth to send him on his way? Because I found him butt naked with my daughter – who is a few months shy of her sixteenth birthday and in an extreme state of undress. So at the very least, I can bring charges of statutory rape."

"Statutory rape? You will have to prove it first."

"Oh I can prove it alright. My daughter will go into a witness box and swear on oath that he forced her into a state of undress. And I doubt very much if he has shown you the cane mark across his obnoxious butt.

"Statutory rape, Laura, and the onus is on your despicable son to disprove it. And by the way, if you feel like calling my bluff and taking this to court, please go ahead and do so. You have my blessing. But then it would come out in evidence what a really bad mother you are. I know what kind of a racket you are running. Did you know you were under silent police investigation because of your high class call girl racket? And it also involves the taking of photographs and thus leaving clients open to blackmail. And Mr. John Smythe? Isn't that the name of the guy you go to see at the Star Five Motel in Greenwich, Connecticut on a weekly basis? And how much does he pay you for your services? Every time you do this, Laura, you cross the state line and commit a federal offence. I know more about federal law than most people, Laura, so don't you dare ever threaten me with court action again. Now I suggest you get the hell off my property and don't come back."

She banged the roof of the car hard with her clenched fist and Laura Benito drove off, wondering just how Athenia de Francia had got the information on her call girl side line. How could she have got it with so many buffer zones between her and her girls and their clients? How could she have possibly known of her weekly Tuesday dalliances (which paid her a handsome sum of pocket money)? She had to stop the car further along the street and she opened the car door to be physically sick into the gutter. She watched it slowly crawl down the drain and felt at this moment this was the way her life was suddenly going and all because her son, her baby, couldn't keep his dick where it should for the time being remain. But she swore vengeance on Athenia de Francia. She was a very patient woman.

****

Susanne-Marie soon forgot Robbie Benito. He had graduated with high marks but he missed the graduation because Laura had packed him off to college earlier than expected.

Susanne-Marie was under curfew for a long, long time – apart from the six months she spent at an expensive boarding school (but she was expelled so soon – the head of the school wrote in her letter to Athenia that such abominable behaviour as displayed by her daughter would not be tolerated at her school) and Athenia was never able to look at her again without a feeling of total mistrust.

But it did not stop Susanne-Marie from making other plans. She had no intentions of being a prissy Mrs. Average

American wifey in this land of the free. She bided her time and then an opportunity by the name of Jeff Klein came into view. Why hadn't she noticed him before? Perhaps it was because he was slow in growing into his manhood but now, it seemed, he was taking off like a rocket. Or perhaps it was because she had wasted so much time on Robbie Benito, that schmuck who didn't know the first thing about girls, that she hadn't noticed Jeff.

****

[1]Jeff Klein was at the height of his self-confidence with the female of the species and he had danced with Susanne-Marie all night, chatted comfortably with her, laughed with her, courted her all evening and the crowd of students from New Rochelle High concentrated more on them than they did the King and Queen of the Graduation Ball – the guys because they were insanely jealous of Jeff succeeding where each of them had failed, and their dates for the evening because their guys were not giving them their fullest attention – and this night had so far been the culmination of his wildest dreams of Susanne-Marie.

For months, she had been the sole object of his youthful sexual fantasies and he knew the strange and dangerously unnatural thoughts he was having of her would never leave him alone: they were too deeply rooted in his subconscious. Every waking moment of the day he thought of her, wondered who she was dating, who she might be sleeping with (*if* she was sleeping with anybody and he hated whoever the low life punk was, the goddamn lucky son of a bitch) and wondered what she looked like without her clothes on, making love to him and only him. He only

---

[1] This section relating to the New Rochelle High Graduation Ball and Susanne-Marie's attempt to seduce Jeff Klein first appeared in Twilight's Last Gleaming, by Jack Walsh and published by Amazon and Kindle.

learned to bring some degree of control to these destructively insane thoughts when he realised he was taking the long route home from school via the wide and tree lined boulevard on which she lived with her parents, hoping beyond hope he just might catch a fleeting glimpse of her or 'accidentally' bump into her (the fact that he saw her at least a dozen times a day at school never entered his head).

He would daydream about her (though in the later stages of this (at present) one-sided relationship, he was careful not to allow the obsession to interfere too much with his studying), think up little fantasies, sketches, one act plays, where they would be alone together and the things they would do to each other and with each other and at the end of it, when coming back into the world of reality – mentally destructive as this was – he would experience such a painfully exciting and sensitive erection he would have to go somewhere private and out of the way to relieve the tension and quite often, his orgasm would be so violent, so powerful and electrified with tension, he had to bite himself on his wrist quite hard to stop himself from screaming out with the pain-pleasure of extracting complete satisfaction.

He was leaving class one afternoon and he passed her as she was walking out the main entrance. He knew none of the guys had been successful in dating her for the Graduation Ball (this had been their sole topic of conversation for the past couple of weeks because every guy had asked her and she had turned down every one of them – including Roberto Benito, the school Romeo) and without even thinking about it, and quite spontaneously, he said to her, "Hi, Suse. I hear through the grapevine that with only three days to go, you still haven't found an escort to the Graduation Ball. Are you going and are you still looking for someone to take you?"

"Hi, Jeff. Yes I am and yes I am."

"You mean you have turned down every guy who has

asked you?" – as if he didn't know already.

"Perhaps they don't measure up to my requirements."

"That's just too bad. Listen, I'll get my cab to pick you up around seven-thirty on the night and we'll see if I measure up. Okay?"

She took two seconds to think about it, appreciated his brash confidence, briefly flashed her brilliantly white teeth in her teasing spider's smile and said, "Okay. Why not?"

She left him standing wide-eyed and open-mouthed and when he finally came back to awareness, he walked home with his head so high in the clouds, he didn't want to come back down to solid ground.

****

They left the Graduation Ball together soon after the last dance and he just knew every pair of eyes were upon him, all insanely jealous of his incredible luck and wishing they could take his place. He revelled in every moment of it. But he was drunk and didn't realise it until they got out of the cab into the cool night air at the North end of the boulevard and walked to her home. He wasn't staggeringly drunk, just light-headed and he began to wish he had stuck to orange juice or soda fizz or something like that instead of drinking strong alcohol just to try and impress her – Hell, why do I need to impress her? She's my date for tonight and she's hot for a good time!

He thought she might be drunk; she acted as if she was but it was really only an act just to give him the come-on: nobody was going to stick one in her while she was senseless from drink. The guys were always telling him she was nothing but a cock teaser but he convinced himself they were only saying that because this dark-complexioned Spanish – American beauty wouldn't date any of them.

Even if she was a cock teaser, he didn't care. She was all over him when they occasionally stopped in the street to give each other slobbering kisses and his hands would brush against the softness of her breasts and her hands would temptingly wander to and grope the growing bulge in his pants.

They stopped in the driveway of her parents' home and he started kissing her and mauling her again, but she resisted.

"No, Jeff, not out here. It's getting cold and I feel so uncomfortable fooling around out here. People might be watching us. Why don't we go inside for coffee – " – and she flashed her spider's smile again – " – or something?"

He couldn't fail to see the tantalising look in her eyes when she said it. The inflexion in her voice made it obvious what she wanted and he knew this was it, but he didn't quite know what to do or say next. He didn't want to mess things up by agreeing too quickly and eagerly to her invitation. He thought it might put her off and besides, she just might be stringing him along in a 'find-out-what-he-does-girly-game'. Now was the time to find out if she really was the cock teaser everybody said she was.

"Well – I don't know – " – looking casually at his watch – " – it's getting late and I don't want your old man going mental and kicking my ass out of the house in the early hours like I was the goddamn pussy cat."

"It's okay, my folks are away for the weekend. Really, they are. They won't be back until late on Sunday. I'm supposed to have the daughter of one of our neighbours around to stay the weekend and look after me while they're gone. Maybe they don't trust me alone in the house. But I called her earlier and told her she should come round tomorrow morning instead because I was sleeping over at the house of one of my girl friends. But you can look after me tonight, can't you. Jeff? You do know how to look after a girl, don't you?" She ran her tongue across his throat and gently sucked on his skin with her soft and moist lips.

"Well – yes – I -"

She leaned close to him and tugged lightly on his ear with her teeth and whispered, "Then there really is no problem. Is there?"

Again, there was that tantalising look in her eyes and he knew he couldn't resist falling into her spider's trap. She took his hand in hers and began to coax him toward the house and into the world of his wildest dreams.

They went into the house and the sudden flow of warm air from the warmth of the central heating of the house against the cool air of the late night made him feel dizzy and in his semi-drunken haze, he could feel the room begin to rotate so very slightly and he fought like a mad dog to remain calm and conscious, but he teetered close to the edge and he just knew he was going to lose the battle.

He remembered her standing at the other end of the room, a teasing and mischievous look in her brilliantly blue eyes. She turned on the radiogram to a low volume, just to give the atmosphere some background sound, and put on a disc. It was Frank Sinatra singing *I've Got You Under My Skin* (a very appropriate choice, she thought) and Nelson Riddle was leading the orchestra.

She kicked off her shoes and said, "Why don't we forget the coffee for now, Jeff? Why don't you come over here and undress me?"

He didn't expect her to be so forward and he remembered thinking that if this was what cock teasing was like, then he wanted more of it. Her request completely threw him for a few seconds and when he regained his composure, he said, "Excuse me? What – what did you say?"

"I said to come over here and undress me. Watch my lips, Jeff. I – want – you – to – come – over – here – and – undress – me! I want you to help me take my clothes off. You know – strip me. You do know what the word 'strip' means, don't you? It means to remove your clothes – or in this case, my clothes. That's what you want, isn't it? To strip me and see what I look like when I'm naked?"

"Yes – I guess - "

"Well, come on then."

He heard what she was saying but he couldn't believe it. He simply could not believe this incredible luck he was experiencing. This was a dream, a cruel dream, and he would wake up in his own bed and be sad that it hadn't really happened. This was the kind of thing people wrote about in cheap and trashy romance or detective novels and he stood rooted to the spot, eyes bulging, mouth hanging wide open and his lips tried to form words but he was struck dumb and could say nothing.

She stood with her long and slender fingers resting lightly on her hips, waiting for him to say something or to make at least one positive move. When she got no reaction from him, she said, "Never mind, Jeff, I'll do it myself. There really is nothing to it. It's so easy when you know how."

She reached behind her neck, unhooked the clasp of her ball gown, messed with the zip at the back and allowed it to slip down to her ankles. She kicked it away and then unhooked her brassiere (he drew in his breath sharply as her overdeveloped breasts flopped down over her chest), slipped off her briefs, nylons and garter belt, so slowly and provocatively, it was like she was doing it to the rhythm of a sensual blues number and he thought: Oh God, if cock teasing be the food of love, give me excess of it (parodying a Shakespearian quotation). But he could feel himself struggling to keep away from the edge of oblivion.

He was dimly aware of her breasts swaying gently from side to side as she came to him and she reached out to help him undress and when her fingers touched his flesh, it was like an electric shock going through his every nerve.

"All I wanted you to do, Jeff, was to remove my clothes. Did you see how easy it was for me to do it? But never mind that now. I want you to do things to me, Jeff – " – as she began to remove the last of his clothes – " – I want you to bring me to such an orgasm I will scream and scream for mercy. You can do that for me, can't you? Do you think you can make me scream that one word, that one very simple word, when I'm having my orgasm? When I'm lying naked beneath you and have you all the way inside me and you have me writhing like a fucking bucking bronco? You can do anything you want with me, Jeff. You know that, don't you? " She kissed him and sucked at the soft flesh around his throat and the sides of his neck and – "Wouldn't you like to take a strap to my ass like my mother does when I misbehave? Wouldn't you like to show me what you can do with a very bad girl like me?"

He was naked and holding on to consciousness for dear life. His hands reached instinctively for the softness of her eighteen year old legs, a smidgen overripe with puppy fat but beautiful nonetheless, and he just knew he would come off before he wanted to, even if she so much as lightly touched his erection with her soft and slender fingers. But she touched it anyway and took it lightly in her open palm, raised it ever so slightly and let it rest against her stomach so she could move closer to him and encircle his neck with her arms.

Nothing else mattered except now and she looked and felt so beautiful and sensual and she radiated all of the voluptuousness he had dreamed of and he dug his fingers into the flesh of her ass as she stuck her tongue deep inside his mouth.

The drink, the mixing of bourbon and wine and Martini, was getting the better of him and he wished to Christ he had stayed sober so he could act out his fantasies on her, but he was losing the fight and her tongue sloshing around inside his mouth was driving him crazy. Then she withdrew it and – "Do things to me, Jeff. Do things to me because I am a very, very naughty girl with some really bad thoughts and I need you to take care of me. Come on, Jeff. Do all of those dirty things you always wanted to do to me. I've seen you watching me. I've seen you walking past the house after school. I've seen the bulge of your dick in your pants when you're thinking about me being naked and lustful. I've seen that look from dozens of the guys at school but it's you I want, Jeff. You won the first prize, everything you have always dreamed of doing to me and with me. Kiss me all over. All over, Jeff. Anywhere. Anywhere you want and for as long as you want. Do dirty things to me. Come and taste the nectar."

And her lips and tongue slid across his throat, down his chest and stomach and she dropped to her knees and ever so lightly took him between the index finger and thumb of her right hand and played her tongue and her beautiful red lips along its entire length and he groaned in sheer ecstasy as he grabbed handfuls of her long brunette hair and desperately tried to hang on to the last thin strands of consciousness remaining to him.

He desperately tried to withhold his imminent orgasm until the very last possible moment and she pushed back his foreskin so delicately, he felt he could no longer hold back. His breath started coming in short gasps and Susanne-Marie rolled her tongue and lips around the tip of his erection and he groaned louder and clasped his hands together behind her head to pull her closer to him. He said her name over and over and she responded eagerly as she took him entirely in her mouth and massive electric shock waves shot through him as her long-nailed fingers dug deeply into the flesh of his thighs and her tongue and lips worked on him until he could stand it no longer.

He remembered screaming long and loud as she suddenly let him go and his orgasm was about to explode and she lay back on the deep-piled carpet, openly inviting him to enter her and act out his wildest fantasies on her. His last conscious thought was that he had never experienced such wild ecstasy before and even as the thought was being processed in his drink-addled brain, the floor suddenly jumped up and smacked into his face.

Susanne-Marie got to her knees and looked down at Jeff lying flat out and unconscious on the carpet and her bitter disappointment knew no bounds.

"You cheated me, you bastard. You cheated me!"

Her frustration, fired by long days and nights of subterfuge, strategy and plot worthy of a vast romantic novel and excited by her seething sexual lust for this beautiful example of male youth, was suddenly outstripped by her feeling of utter deflation at being thwarted at the point of no return.

She lay herself flat on the carpet, briefly touched herself and howled and screamed and orgasmed out of control.

A few days later, Jeff sent her a letter saying how sorry he was he had messed things up and asked for another chance. But she never even gave him the courtesy of a reply, being far too busy trying to work her teenage womanly wiles on the Captain of the school football team, who became her next willing victim in her gossamer web.

Eventually, Jeff grew up, married and went to Vietnam and put Susanne-Marie to the back of his mind: gone but not quite forgotten.

****

Athenia bumped into her friend's daughter, Lucy, a few days later while she was out shopping in the town.

"Hi, Lucy. While you're here, I owe you some money for looking after Susanne-Marie. Let's see, two nights, Friday and Saturday, and two days, Saturday and Sunday at ten dollars each and that is forty dollars I owe you."

"It's only thirty, Mrs. De Francia. Susanne-Marie told me she was sleeping at a friend's house on Friday evening and told me not to bother to come round."

"And which friend would that be?"

"She was staying with Joanne Bascombe. She was back home by the time I arrived at ten Saturday morning. And as I was going in, a young man came out. Must have been her boyfriend. He looked like he was having one doozy of a hangover too."

Athenia didn't believe Susanne-Marie had stayed over with a friend and as far as her daughter was concerned, she could smell a rat even if it had bathed in the most expensive perfume Paris had to offer. When she got home later in the day, she called Joanne Bascombe's house and spoke directly to Joanne.

"Joanne, I have a question to ask you. Did Susanne-Marie have a sleepover with you last Friday evening?"

"No, Mrs. De Francia. She was going to but she cancelled and came to the Prom with one of the guys from school. Went home with him too. Oh dear, have I said something wrong?"

"No, that's just fine. I just wanted to clear up an anomaly. Thank you, Joanne."

Athenia had an errand to take care of and on her return, she met Susanne-Marie at the front entrance of the house. She was about to depart for a meeting with friends when Athenia stopped her.

"Back inside, missy. I want words with you."

She shoved her back inside the house when she started to object and led her by a firm grip on her arm to her study upstairs.

"Let go my arm, mother, you're hurting me."

"Well, isn't that a shame? It's only in return for you hurting me."

"I don't understand. What is this about?"

"You were supposed to have Lucy stay with you last Friday night. You told her you were taking a sleepover with a friend. Joanne Bascombe? I spoke to Joanne and she said the last she saw of you Friday evening was leaving the graduation ball with a young man. So first of all, you have lied to me. Secondly, you have lied to Lucy and thirdly, I suspect you had a boy staying the night with you. So an explanation please."

"Okay, so I had someone stay the night. But nothing happened because he was drunk and he passed out and slept the night on the floor. Nothing happened, mother. I will swear an oath on that. He really did sleep on the carpet all night and left the next morning with his hangover."

"Well judging by your past record – and you haven't been that long home from boarding school – I would say that you swearing an oath would be tantamount to perjury. And thus I can only believe you had this boy over to stay and you got up to God alone knows what filthy perversions. So what, Susanne-Marie, do you think we ought to do about this latest bout of your bad behaviour?"

Athenia smiled when she said this but Susanne-Marie failed to notice the lack of motherly kindness in her eyes and thus she smiled in return when she replied, "I don't know. Do you want me butt naked again so you can give me a good thrashing – so you can have yourself another cheap thrill?"

Athenia swung her hand as far back as she could and brought it round to slap her face so hard, it knocked her off her feet.

"How dare you speak to me like that. How goddamn dare you! This is not a subject to smirk and smile about. I asked you a question – what do you propose I do about this disgusting incident? What do I do about those disgusting and abhorrent thoughts lying in your head like some filthy stagnant pool of dirt?"

And then the strength of Susanne-Marie surprised even Athenia when she suddenly got up, grabbed her by the throat and dragged her outside onto the stairs landing and hung her head over the bannister.

"Listen, mother dearest. If I want to go out partying, drinking and fucking and have a general good time, I will do precisely that. If I want to bring a guy home and let him fuck the ass off me, I will do precisely that. But Friday night, nothing happened in the way you think. But I'll tell you something, mother dearest. I sucked his cock, right down to the roots, and I enjoyed every last second of it!"

"Don't you dare use such gutter language in this house! Heaven alone knows where you got that from!"

"What words don't you like mother – words like cock and fuck? What about tits or fellatio? You can find those words in any respectable dictionary you know. Just look once in a while and stop being such a goddamned old maid. How old are you? Thirty-seven? You act like you were an eighty year old grandmother lost in the wrong time period."

"Get out of this house, Susanne-Marie. Get out and

stay out until you can learn some respect!"

"Okay, mommy dearest. Guess I'll go and drink myself stupid among other things – which I won't mention because you are so hung up on sex – and I'll come back home when I've had my fill."

But she went back into her room, slammed the door in her mother's face and didn't emerge until the next day.

****

At some time over the next few months, they decided on a truce, Athenia believing that if Susanne-Marie was having as hard a time becoming a woman as she had had, well, she didn't like her attitude but she accepted it as the girl's own problems with maturing into adulthood.

The truce between mother and teenage daughter was a delicate balance between saying the right thing and not laying down the law in a parental fashion, and accepting the fact that Susanne-Marie was growing into a woman and things were never going to be as easy as it said in the text books.

And then at some time during the next eighteen months, the truce gradually disintegrated and became a situation of bare tolerance by each of them to the other. Sometimes, they tended to treat each other like a pair of back alley tom cats encircling each other and about to start their own war of attrition, yet at other times, the atmosphere was cool but pleasant enough but both realised that this could not go on for ever. It sent Athenia into fits of deep depression from which she never really recovered and which tended to lay dormant but dangerously alive at the back of her mind. She knew she was losing her grip on her home and her place within it as the matriarch who must not be disobeyed and from that point on, she tended to look at her past, present and future life with the very profoundest of Swiftian motives.

****

For some reason – and mayhap there were plenty if the three occupants of the house decided to delve deeply enough – the marriage between Athenia and Tomas began to disintegrate. It wasn't a rapid decline but it was slow and mildly painful (at first) but it slowly began to get ugly. It was like woodworm infesting the beams of a house: things started happening, things at first unnoticeable but there when reminded, but there was a definite desire of whatever was controlling their lives to see it through to the bitter end. It seemed as if all three, Tomas, Athenia and Susanne-Marie, were doomed to utter destruction as a single entity within the house and by the time any one of them saw it coming, it was too late to put matters into a reverse gear.

****

On Thursday May 2 1958, Athenia saw Alessandro Lucania one final time before she dispensed with his services. Laura Benito and her family had moved out of New Rochelle soon after her spat with Athenia and now lived closer to New York City in the North Riverdale District of the Bronx. Lucania had been retained on an on and off basis by Athenia to carry out jobs to gather evidence in difficult cases and he always came up with the goods.

He came to her office one day in the spring of 1958 to collect his monthly cash payment but then made a serious and, for him, fatal error of judgement.

He took his envelope of cash and said, "Before I go, I think you ought to know that your friend Laura Benito has surfaced again."

"Oh? What is it to do with me? I have no further interest in Laura Benito."

"She will be of interest to you because she is still playing her old games and I have a list of her clients."

"And why should that be of interest to me? By the way, is she still under investigation?"

"Yes she is. There has been renewed interest in her file which has been gathering dust for a few years. Lack of evidence. Until now, that is. But this list of clients. There are six names on the list. Laura Benito is blackmailing each of the names on the list because she has compromising photographs of them. Photographs - you know the kind of thing I mean."

"I'm getting tired of this conversation. Come to the point."

"Your husband is on the list and Laura Benito is blackmailing him."

"Over what?"

"I told you – compromising photographs."

"What kind of compromising photographs?"

"Photographs involving hookers – some as young as fourteen, fifteen or sixteen."

"How do you know all of this?"

"Because one of the girls she uses is prepared to turn state's evidence against Laura Benito."

"And what do you expect me to do about it?"

"I'll come straight to the point, Mrs. De Francia. I expect a very large payment. A payment for my silence and the photographs."

Athenia thought for a while.

"How much?"

"Well. I'm not a greedy man so let's say fifty thousand dollars will be enough to buy my silence. It also buys Laura Benito's silence too."

"You work for her as well as for me?"

"Let's just say we are acquainted."

"And why should I trust either of you?"

"You either trust us or bear the extreme discomfort of knowing your husband has been found cavorting with under age females. That carries a prison sentence you know. And on several occasions, he has crossed a state line to do what he likes doing with these young girls. That is a federal offence and he's well and truly hooked. It's like he's taking candy from a nickel bag. A federal offence, Mrs. De Francia."

"Don't quote the law at me, Mr. Lucania. What else do I get for my fifty thousand dollars? Besides your silence, that is."

"All the photographs and the negatives."

"And Laura Benito hands them all over to me for a one off payment of fifty thousand dollars?"

"We aren't greedy so you will have to trust us on this."

"Why should I comply? Why don't I just call your bluff?"

"That's entirely up to you but the fifteen year old girl who is going to turn state's evidence on Laura Benito? At the moment, she's in hiding, arranged by the State Prosecutor's office. But she means business. She isn't just threatening to do it – she *will* do it. If that happens, it means a jury will see all of the evidence, including the photographs of your husband. It'll finish you, Mrs. De Francia. Within the New York legal fraternity, it'll finish you."

Athenia thought a few moments on this and then said, "Alright, I agree. Let's see, today is Thursday. Come and see me here on Saturday morning at ten and I will have your money ready for you."

"In used notes and none any higher than a twenty."

"I will comply with that. And I trust you will have the photographs and negatives with you?"

"I'll have them."

"Goodbye, Mr. Lucania."

He got up from his chair and left Athenia's office and the building. By the time he stepped out on to the sidewalk, the smirk had still not cleared from his face.

On Friday May 3 1958 at four in the morning, Alessandro Lucania was found with a bullet to the back of his head. It had been made to look like (and indeed it was) a gangland execution.

Later on the same day, Laura Benito was found dead in her apartment in Riverdale, a bullet to the back of her head. It had been made to look like (and indeed it was) a gangland execution.

Police discovered that her safe had been opened but they had no idea what might have been taken. The killer, also an expert safecracker, had removed thirty thousand dollars in cash, a number of negatives to some extremely embarrassing photographs, the photographs to go with the negatives and a small account book with names on each of several pages, one of which belonged to Tomas de Francia.

When it was thought that the two killings might be connected, a comparison was made of the bullets but it was discovered they had been fired by different guns, one a .38 Colt and the other a .38 Beretta.

When Athenia met with a certain Sicilian gentleman at her office on Saturday morning, being the thoroughly honest person he was, he handed over all he had taken from the safe.

"I only want the photographs and corresponding negatives, Mr. Siracusa. The thirty thousand dollars I haven't seen but keep it as a bonus. And here is your ten thousand dollar fee. I am most grateful for your services."

"Thank you, Mrs. De Francia. If you should need my services again, you know how to contact me."

"I will bear that in mind and thank you so much for your services and your time over the past few days."

****

Tomas came home and Athenia was moving furniture into a spare bedroom.

"What are you doing?" he said.

"I'm moving a bed into the spare room so I can sleep in peace at night."

Tomas didn't detect the bitterness in her answer and he joked, "Oh, I didn't realise I snored so loud. Shall we discuss it?"

"What is there to discuss?"

"You're serious about this, aren't you?"

"You bet I am. And let's get one thing very clear. Where would you be if it wasn't for me? Some two bit attorney in a run down office? Everything you are now in the legal profession you owe to me and that is all you are going to get from me. And if moving my bedroom is going to keep your grubby little hands away from me, so much the better. I certainly do not want any more children and as far as doing it for fun and pleasure is concerned I find it an extremely abhorrent and filthy practice and I have no interest in it any further."

"Athenia, what has got into you? What has brought this on all of a sudden?"

And then she turned on him. "Do you really want to know? Do you want to know that I have found out the truth about you?"

"I don't know what you're talking about."

"How much did you pay Laura Benito? In blackmail money? Don't answer that because I know how much you paid her. She kept an account book with a page especially for each person she was blackmailing. You paid her fifteen thousand dollars over the last six months. Don't worry, no one else is going to find out about it. I have the book locked away in a bank vault."

"I…I don't know what to say. It was all a mistake."

"What was a mistake? Letting Laura Benito get the better of you or being caught fucking under age girls? I have the black and white photographs plus the negatives to prove it and they are locked away with the account book."

"Athenia, I can explain."

"Don't bother. If you went with hookers, I could understand it. It's a man thing and they think it's great to try and get one over on wifey at home. But under age girls? Jesus Christ but you committed a criminal offence every time you went with one of them! Girls younger than your own daughter, for Christ's sake! Didn't you once consider your own family and the embarrassment it would bring us if you were found out?

"And you crossed the state line several times too. You really ought to have known better crossing a state line to have sex with a minor. When does it stop being paedophilia and become just sex with a hooker? Didn't you consider our standing in the legal profession? Or were you just so eager to get your dirty little kicks and to hell with everything and everyone else?

She slapped him hard across the face and stormed out

of the room.

He sat on the bed and hung his head in despair. This was by far the worst day of his life and he had known from the very beginning that it might come to this if he continued with his nasty habits. But he was like a drug addict; he couldn't stop and the efforts he did make to stop were piss-poor efforts and he kept thinking: Just one more time; one more time and I'll quit.

But Laura Benito had him in her spider's web and she started to milk him. It was done purely as an act of revenge against Athenia for humiliating her when she complained to her about assaulting her son.

But Athenia let her husband stew in his own guilt and corruption. Let him sweat it out, she thought. He'll find out soon enough that he is safe from Laura Benito, that venomous damned tarantula bitch. And if you want your fifteen thousand dollars back, your shit out of luck because I gave it to someone as a bonus.

Tomas wept silently in his room and Athenia slept in a separate room with a Cheshire cat grin on her face. But the grin held no pleasure: it was evil and in her sleep, it had taken her over. The madness which fed it gradually fed on her until it had complete control.

****

The good feeling that she had dealt with some of her enemies – and her husband – didn't last for very long. Athenia began drinking heavily and it seemed she didn't care about where it might be leading her. She drifted ever more frequently into bouts of serious depression from which it seemed impossible to lift herself, but they eventually went of their own accord, only to return days or weeks later to torment her once more.

People at her law practice began to desert her employ because clients were going elsewhere. Friends started deserting her because she would turn up drunk at parties, cause trouble and on one occasion, she was requested to leave someone's house, she was so drunk and abusive.

Wilma Vernon was humiliated in her own home by Athenia when, drunk on whatever she could grab to drink, she had yelled out that Wilma was a committed member of the Communist Party and the Committee on un-American activities would soon be kicking her front door in with an arrest warrant.

And Tomas fed his addiction with constant promises to himself that he would quit but knowing deep within himself that this was an impossibility. He was hooked, he was addicted, like a junkie to heroin, and he couldn't stop. He didn't seem to care. He had heard that Laura Benito had been murdered and his smugness knew no bounds. At least she wouldn't be bothering him again and if Athenia knew what he had been up to, so what? If she wants to sleep in a different room and a different bed, I'm not bothered.

He was closer to Laura Benito than Athenia thought because she had introduced him to some very high class girls a long time ago. If the price was right, they would do anything the human heart desired but he soon began to tire of the same old thing (he just knew some of them faked orgasm and thus he felt cheated and the play-acting roles seemed to be like a cheaply made Hollywood B movie) and when Laura suggested someone younger, he went for it like a rat in a drainpipe.

The chick was fifteen and looked beautiful; not dressed up like a doll or made up to look older, but she was fifteen and looked so virginal and pure. It was the way he liked them.

He knew he was breaking the law and if he was ever found out, it would mean a prison sentence (serious probation at the very least) and it would take care of his marriage and his career too. But he couldn't resist. He couldn't resist the total innocence of some of these girls – but some of them had very vivid imaginations and really knew how to boogey.

He revelled in it. It was a drug and he was hooked and he reached the stage where he didn't care who found out. He had eaten of the forbidden fruit and he was well and truly hooked.

Sometimes, he wanted things to go a little deeper than just straight man on top sex and for the right fee, they were more than willing to comply. Either they had college fees to pay or a drugs habit to fund (or they simply liked the power they held over these men and thus made them pay for it). He liked them to give hand jobs, blow jobs; he liked to spank them and play the stern father figure. He paid the money and they complied with whatever he wanted.

And Laura Benito continued to take the black and white photographs, keep the negatives and total the payments in her very private ledger.

****

Tomas' favourite tootsy had given him the cold shoulder because she said he was too weird and if he came near her again, she would tell the cops. She told him she had heard things about him from a few of the other girls and she didn't like what she heard.

And so he went home instead of to the law practice and just hung around his bedroom drinking whiskey and slowly becoming drunker and angrier.

Susanne-Marie came home at lunchtime from her college course to begin a long weekend. She was bored; bored with her friends, bored with her college course (Secretarial Administration) and she was bored with life in general. After Jeff Klein, there had been no one special; a few short relationships which had gone nowhere and were never really intended to go anywhere at all. Jeff had gone off to West Point and what came after that, she didn't know. She guessed in later years he might have gone to Vietnam.

Dumbass bitch, she thought to herself. You're pining after him. No, I am not. Yes, you *are*! He cheated you on that one night and it was a while before you forgave him but when you were ready for him again, he had flown the nest.

Tomas was in his bedroom still and Susanne-Marie went up the stairway. She heard the clink of a glass and bottle on a metal tray as she passed Tomas' room. She walked in and saw him slouching in a chair with a glass of whiskey in his hand and a half empty bottle of the stuff on the silver tray atop the bedside table.

"What are you doing home so early?" she asked him.

"I haven't been to the office. Decided to stay home and get drunk instead."

"Why?"

"Why? Your goddamn mother, that's why. Moving out of the marital bedroom just because I made a few silly mistakes. I should be master in my own home but I am not – and it's all because of that infernal bitch!"

"So what did you do?"

"I was unfaithful with a few women is all. What's so wrong about that? Thousands…millions of guys do it all the time. I never meant anything by it. They never meant anything to me. So why?"

"Don't ask me. I really don't care. Cry into your bottle of whiskey because you won't get sympathy anywhere in this house."

She had not correctly gauged the depth of his seething anger and like a pouncing leopard, Tomas leaped up from the bed, grabbed Susanne-Marie by her hair and slapped her face, then punched her a few times in the face and when she went down, he kicked her a few times. She was strong, but Tomas was stronger, such strength fuelled by the drink and his seething anger at his wife and the bitch who wanted to call the cops on him and now his own daughter telling him it was all tough shit.

"Don't talk to me like I'm nothing!" he yelled as she lay on the floor, legs and arms splayed, half in and out of consciousness and this enraged him even more. More than that, it inflamed him. He went for the kill.

****

Athenia could – *smell*! – something. It was something evil; she couldn't at first find the right word to define it because the smell only existed in her imagination – but it was disgusting. Whatever was wrong had a stink so evil, she could hardly bear it. It was there, in the atmosphere of the house, and it was not her imagination after all.

She started to walk very slowly up the stairs, sniffing unconsciously at the air, as if she were following this obnoxious odour of corruption like a sniffing dog. But she could smell it. It hung in the air like a cloying and disgusting stench from an age-old sewer and it made her gut wrench several times, but she knew it was only in her imagination. But imagination did not solve the problem of what the smell was. And then she got it: it was the smell of base human corruption.

She heard a soft moaning coming from Tomas' bedroom and she slowly pushed the door open. Tomas was naked and so was Susanne-Marie and he was on top of her and engaged in an incestuous act of sex and she had her legs wrapped round him like she was hanging on for dear life and she started bucking like a wild horse and her moans of ecstasy grew in crescendo as Tomas went deeper into her and neither Tomas nor Susanne-Marie realised Athenia was standing at the door watching them with a screwed up face of pure and utter disgust. They didn't know. They didn't know!

She moved quietly away, went to the bathroom and was violently sick to the extent that for a long, long time, she could not stop retching. When she had finally finished, her rib cage felt as if it had been used as a professional boxer's punchbag.

Susanne-Marie staggered from her father's bedroom (he had been hitting her all the time they were making love because it excited him to do it – but Susanne-Marie had had enough) and collapsed into her mother's arms. Athenia called an ambulance, which took her to a private hospital. Remarkably, when Athenia returned home the next day, Tomas was still at home and still drinking.

Bastard, she thought. He didn't even have the guts or common sense to run for his life.

Late on Saturday evening (she hadn't spoken to Tomas all day and he still hung around the house as if nothing had happened – but he remained in his room drinking, sleeping, going from sober to drunk to sober and drunk, over and over: it was a never ending carousel of alcoholic oblivion) Athenia got herself ready to retire to bed but then went downstairs; she felt a massive headache looming and she wanted medication before it took a hold. While in the kitchen, she took a long carving knife from one of the drawers. She didn't know why she did this; she simply picked the knife from the drawer. She was also in the throes of an excessively deep depression and she knew this one was not going to go away as easily as the others had seemed to. Although those others had been bad, she just knew this one was here to stay for a long, long time. She went back upstairs and into Tomas' room. He was snoring softly on the bed and she could smell the drink on him.

She shook him. "Wake up, Tomas, you dirty bastard. Wake up. We need to talk."

"What…whaddya want? Leave me alone." He turned over slightly and closed his eyes in sleep.

"I saw you and her yesterday afternoon when I came back from the office."

He had fallen back into a light sleep and didn't hear her.

Athenia went into the bathroom and filled a plastic bucket with cold water, went back to Tomas' room and threw it over him.

"What the hell are you doing?" he yelled as he suddenly jack-knifed into a sitting position. "Leave me the hell alone! Oh God! Look what you've done!"

"We need to talk, Tomas." She swung her fist and hit him directly on the jaw. It put him out for a few minutes but it was sufficient time for her to take four lengths of silk cord and tie his wrists and ankles to the upper and lower bedposts.

"Did any of your young hookers ever do this for you?" she said when he came round and saw he was utterly helpless. He could tell by the insane look on Athenia's face and the evil smile on her lips that this was not going to be a husband and wife sex game on a Saturday evening.

"I know they did because I've seen the photographs. Only it was you tying them down. Let's see how you cope when the roles are reversed.

"There will be no respite for you today, this evening or ever because there is something serious we have to get through. There is no way out of this for either of us, especially for you. I saw you and Susanne-Marie together yesterday afternoon. I doubt if you can explain your way out of this one but you might as well try."

And then he suddenly came out of his semi-drunken stupor and understood.

"Athenia, what happened with Susanne-Marie was a mistake. I...I don't know what to...see, she came on to me and there was nothing I could do."

"You lying bastard. She said you hit her a number of times in the face, both slapped her and punched her and kicked her, stripped her and raped her. When I came home yesterday, I saw the two of you together but you were on top of her and she looked completely out of it, although she had her legs wrapped around you. And you were hitting her still. Do you know what I did when I saw you fucking your own daughter? I went into the bathroom and threw up my lunch and breakfast and whatever else was inside of me. I'm surprised you didn't hear me and come running to see what you could do to help me."

"Athenia, I swear – on my life, I swear she came on to me."

"You were always a poor liar. I guess she came on to you like all those other young girls you were photographed with. I've seen most of the negatives so don't deny it. I know what kind of practices you have been up to with all of those young girls and you thought you could involve our daughter in the same filthy mud of your dirty mind?"

There was a strange look in Athenia's eyes and a strange half smile across her face. It frightened Tomas because he had never before looked into the face of bare insanity. She let her peignoir slip from her shoulders to the floor, but she still had a firm grasp of the carving knife.

"How do I look to you, Tomas? Do I look beautiful? As beautiful as the day we got married? Did I excite you on our first night alone? Well, do you like me? Am I still the woman you married? Do I still look beautiful to you? Have I retained enough of my youthful figure to excite you? Do you feel as if you could make love to me all night like we used to? But that didn't last very long, did it? I suppose as I started to get older, you were even then hankering after something young and sprightly and virginal and innocent."

She then straddled him and sat on his knees so he couldn't move. He was completely and utterly in her power and this was precisely the way she wanted him.

She sat on the bed and holding the carving knife between thumb and forefinger, she leaned forward and drew it lightly across his chest from left to right. He watched the knife and not the insane look in her eyes and the evil smile which still adorned her lips.

"I want to tell you something that you have never known, least of all suspected. Six months before we were married, my own father, a minister of the Baptist church, raped me and made me pregnant. I had – my mother insisted on and arranged – an abortion. As a supposed human entity, it was unrecognisable as a human being when it dripped out of me. And you thought you had a virgin for a wedding present? Far from it, husband of mine. My own father had that privilege from me. And years after, I sought out his grave, poured a large bottle of my own piss on it and spat on his grave as much as I could until I had nothing left to spit – but by then, I was satisfied that I had done all I could to wreak my revenge.

"And yesterday, I came home and find you drunk and in the process of engaging in sexual intercourse with our daughter. So this bullshit story about her coming on to you, no, I don't believe that."

And she pressed on the knife and dragged it over his chest to his stomach, scoring a deep cut all the way down. And then she gently pushed the knife into his stomach for several inches and let it remain there. He was still alive.

"Athenia…no…please…no…"

"Shut up, Tomas," and she gently prised the knife out of his stomach, drew the knife across his stomach and further down to his groin, opening up another long wound which bled profusely. She then sliced off his genitalia, shoved it in his screaming mouth and laughed malevolently.

His blood oozed from his wounds and Athenia revelled in drinking his spurting blood and as she leaned forward to puke it back up, she plunged the knife deep into his chest. She could still hear him screaming (even though she knew he was dead) and could not tolerate the sound of it so she kept stabbing and slashing at his chest and stomach and laughing insanely until the screaming noises in her head finally stopped.

****

Susanne-Marie came home from the hospital on Sunday afternoon and when she walked through the front door, she stopped and listened. She could hear smacking / cracking / swishing sounds coming from upstairs and cries of pain.

She walked slowly up the stairway, the sounds getting closer. She walked passed Tomas' bedroom and looked through the open door and saw his blood-soaked body lying on the bed and the knife sticking out of his chest and there was blood soaking the bed linen and there was blood on the walls and everywhere it could splatter. She knew the carving knife well and knew that it was as sharp as sharp could be and that at least eight or nine inches of the blade must be buried in his chest. There was a faint smell of bodily corruption emanating from the room.

She showed no emotion, no shock, no sudden screams of, "OH MY GAAAHHHDDD". No, she walked passed the room and into her mother's bedroom from where the cracking sounds and cries of pain were emanating.

Her mother was naked to the waist and her back was covered in blue and purple weals from where the five-thonged whip had bit into her flesh.

"If thine eye offend thee, then shalt thou pluck it out!" she cried out and struck herself again, and a second and third time until Susanne-Marie took the whip from her.

"Oh God, mother, just look at the state of you! Why are you doing this to yourself? What the hell is it you're in to? Jesus Christ Almighty, you read about this kind of thing in trashy pornographic books."

"You will not take the Lord's name in vain. Not ever in this house."

"Never mind that now – let me see to you. Why are you doing this to yourself? Is this because of what happened on Friday?"

"I'm inflicting punishment because I have to atone for my sins. I should have kept the baby and not let mother take it away from me. Oh God help me because I have sinned against your commandments. Oh Lord, I pray for your forgiveness!"

"What are you talking about, mother? What baby?"

"You dirty, filthy, fucking little slut. Did you enjoy your time with him? Has he made you pregnant with a bastard child? Do you know it will be your brother or sister and it will call you mama?" It wasn't her mother's voice but something strangely and deeply guttural.

Susanne-Marie had no idea what she was talking about. She had never been told of her mother's aborted child all those years ago and now Athenia was rambling and laughing to herself and rambling and shaking and dribbling. In the throes of her destructive headache and deep depression, and finally her madness, she had imagined all sorts of things which may not have been true but which in her mind were very real.

"Shall I tell you what I did when I saw you fucking him? I brought up every meal I had had in the last couple of days, you nymphomaniac slut. Not content with his whores and hookers and under-age little alley cats, he had to soil you. He had to soil you, my precious, precious and only child."

In the deterioration of her sanity, her religious mania was coming to the fore and it increased her wild imagination out of all proportion. But she knew in the depths of her soul what she had seen them doing on Friday afternoon.

"It is all my fault. All of this degradation within my family – I have spread it like a filthy disease and it was all because I let that cursed woman murder my child. And now all the bad things are happening. He raped you because of my sins. You turned against me because of my sins. You depraved yourself God alone knows how many times because of my sins. It was all my fault. Give me back my whip because I have to atone for my wrongdoing."

Susanne-Marie stared closely into her insane face and laughed softly. "Mother, aren't you just a little hung up about sex? Just because you saw him on top of me, you think he raped me? Oh no, mother dearest. Far from it. He never raped me. He started to but it ended up with me making love to him.

"What shall I tell you, mother? That I enjoyed it? Every last second I enjoyed it and I let him go into me all the way as far as he could and I screamed and screamed as I came and came and I sucked his cock, mother! I sucked his cock all the way down to the roots. I let him shove it up my ass! I let him slobber and come all over my very large tits! I fucked him mommy – I fucked him and I enjoyed every last slobbering orgasmic second and oh boy you wouldn't believe the power of what I felt – and even when he was hitting and slapping me around, I had one great big massive orgasm after another and I couldn't stop coming and coming and coming! I let him come all over my face and I drank him and I was – drunk on him. I was very, very drunk on him. But I'll tell the cops he raped me. Is that what you want, mother dearest? Who is going to believe you?"

Susanne-Marie called the police and they were at the house within ten minutes and still around several hours later.

A young, thirty-ish looking detective, Jack Delaney, tried to interview Athenia but she was incoherent and he could barely understand what she was saying except, "I'm not surprised you are still an ordinary detective. You are so naïve, aren't you? Isn't it obvious what happened here? He didn't rape her. I don't care what she told you. He wasn't making love to her – she was making love to him! Please give me my whip because I have to atone for her sins as well as my own. Please, young man."

In his interview with Susanne-Marie, he repeated what Athenia had told him.

"My illustrious mother," she replied, "would not know a good fuck if one stared her in the face. He raped me but it's her fingerprints on the knife. Is that right, she cut off his genitals and shoved them in his mouth? My mother is vicious."

When the police took Athenia away, she was laughing softly to herself. It was weird and frightening.

By the time her trial came to court some few months later, she was a raving lunatic and after listening to police statements and that of Susanne-Marie (she perjured herself in the witness box), psychiatrists, social workers and what have you, Athenia de Francia was thus sentenced to an indeterminate period in a secure mental hospital. She died in the hospital in April of 1971. In one of her brief moments of sanity, she overdosed on the medication she had been saving for a month.

Brooklyn – West Coast – South Bronx: 1960 - 1976

A few months after the trial, Susanne-Marie requested the family attorneys to sell the house on her behalf and put the proceeds in the trust fund Athenia had set up for her some years previously. It stated that from her eighteenth birthday for a period of nine years, the trustees would send her a monthly payment to cover her living expenses. The entire estate would not transfer to her ownership until the age of thirty-five and in any event, this assumed she would be well ensconced in a salaried position and / or in a state of marriage. The estate would pass to any of her children in equal amounts on her death.

She packed her belongings and moved away from New Rochelle. Emilia, Susanne-Marie's aunt and whose father was Jorge and her brother was Tomas, was married to Tony Romano, who ran a small chain of ice cream parlours in Brooklyn and they lived in a brownstone building in Brooklyn Heights. Before Susanne-Marie's solitary move to Brooklyn, she never had much to do with Emilia. But when her mother was taken away and when she wanted to move away from New Rochelle, there was more frequent contact and Emilia found her the apartment close to her home in Brooklyn Heights.

She loved life in Brooklyn Heights. It was clean and fresh and disinfected of the underlying corruption of her existence in New Rochelle. She intended to remain in Brooklyn Heights for a long time to come. She wished to remain anonymous for a while and not be constantly hounded by the gutter press as the daughter of the jealous and insane wife who knifed her husband to death when she discovered he had raped his own daughter. She wanted people around her but not the snobbish and snooty kind her parents (but mainly her mother) had cultivated in New Rochelle, whom, she remembered, had all deserted her at her time of need.

She was happy for a while but then the novelty of being surrounded by ordinary people began to wear off and things slowly but surely began to fall apart.

****

Five years of freedom and she was still trying to define why she had on that day viciously turned against her mother and allowed Tomas to rape / make love to her. She hated what she had said after the event also. She had never hated Tomas up to that point, simply disliked him. She knew he was a sook and under the strong influence of her mother.

But Tomas had been the first. Oh yes, there had been various fumblings, most of them frustratingly disappointing, in the back seats of cars in drive in movie houses and in dark areas of parks where most of the kids hung out Friday and Saturday nights, but until Tomas, there had never been penetration.

Okay, so he had hit her when she taunted him and she fell into a brief state of semi-consciousness when she had hit the floor but she was awake enough to feel Tomas undressing her and he was so woozy from drink and she said, "I've seen the way you look at me sometimes, you dirty bastard. So let's see what you can do with a real woman."

And then he lifted her on to the bed, mounted her and started slapping her face and a few times, he used his fists and when he entered her, their collective wild animal lust knew no bounds and she wrapped her legs around his waist and it seemed they went on for ever, depraving themselves and enjoying each other's wanton lust.

She could never understand why she got so much pleasure from him hitting and slapping her face throughout the ordeal but it only added to the evidence against him that, contrary to Athenia's statement, he had actually raped her.

Athenia was truly a beautiful woman (all of the rottenness on the inside was of no importance; it was the outside which mattered initially) and Susanne-Marie was astute enough to realise that it wasn't her looks that made her so bad, so unattractive to her husband (who, Susanne-Marie thought, was not a bad looking guy after all): perhaps it was the ruthlessness of the businesswoman inside her. She pondered this for years until she was one day going through her mother's paperwork she had left behind and found her diaries.

And perhaps it was the sight of Tomas raping his own daughter (what she at first thought until Susanne-Marie confirmed otherwise) which brought back the memories of her own father raping her. Ethan had been her first and Tomas had soiled his own daughter, he being Susanne-Marie's first also.

Susanne-Marie was physically sick when she read this and soon after fell into a long term spell of seriously deep depressions and decline. She realised she and her mother had fought, sometimes like cat and dog, for several years before Tomas's death. It was something she regretted but dismissed because she could not go back in time to alter the state of things. What was said and done remained said and done.

She wanted something to take away the pain of recent years. She wanted to, but could not, forget and thus, she drifted toward a danger point from which, she fully realised, there may be no return.

She knew there was a drugs market in Brooklyn and she knew some of the guys who ran it and their addicts. It was pitifully easy for her to graduate from the occasional snort of coke to something a little stronger but just as easily come by.

****

Lucius was a black guy popular in the neighbourhood. He was known to deal, had a string of chicks chasing him and he drove a mauve coloured 1959 Cadillac 60 Special with tail end fins and the chrome bead running from front fender to rear bumper. It had a 325 horsepower engine underneath the hood and he was one cool black guy man about town, always had some fine fox on his arm and he didn't deal with just anyone. His skag was the best and it was only for the best. There were no ragged ass dope fiends on his client list.

She knew Lucius vaguely, had seen him hanging around Brooklyn Heights and mayhap wished him, "Hi," occasionally. So when she sat down at his table in a Brooklyn diner, he was curious. She was one class bitch and he was curious. She had style and he was curious. She had – whatchacallit? – pizzazz! Yeah! That's what she had, pizzazz, and he was curious.

Lucius said, "What's a beautiful lookin' babe like you doin' when you wants skag like you think I got? Where you comin' from? What game you playin' with me, my girl?"

"I just want a taste is all. I've got some bad problems and I need a taste."

"Nobody jus' wants a taste and jus' one taste ain't goin' solve whatever problems you got, child. And we all got problems. Mine at the moment is a real expensive divorce but I ain't shootin' shit because I lost my babe. Hell no. I ain't shootin' shit at all. I gots more sense. What you got in the way of problems?"

"That's my business."

"And dope is my bizness. But it don't mean I have to sell it to you."

She got up to go. She was in no mood to tongue-wag with this black feller with the almost permanent smile on his face and his pearly white teeth and his flashing gold jewellery.

"That's okay. There are other people I can buy from."

"Wait. Wait. Wait. Jus' hold yo hosses for a while there, missy. There are cowboys in this town who would no sooner rip you off than look at you. I knows one guy who would sell you one hundred per cent quinine if you looks like a cherry. An' the good stuff? Well, he'll cut it four, five, six times a'fore he even thinks of sellin' it to even the best of his dudes. Now me? I only cut once. Fifty fifty straight down the middle an' use fine sugar jus' so the shit taste an' smell sweet. You don' ever take the pure shit 'less you knows what you doin' an' you looks like a real cherry pie to me, missy. But you don't get no shit house cleaner or rat poison mixed in my skag."

And thus, their brief relationship began. He started selling her heroin (but only to smoke) but in case she wanted to graduate to higher things, he showed her how to cook it and use the syringe.

"I'm only showing you this because the only other way is to learn by your mistakes and mistakes here can be expensive and dangerous. You take too much of this stuff and you gonna get hooked an' one day, it's goin' kill you stone dead."

She learned and very quickly and the first time she took a dose, the hit was almost instantaneous and out of this world. And even then, it was cut straight down the middle with fine sugar, just like he said it was. She kept on getting the good hits and life seemed like an idyll. She once bought some skag from him but she asked for time to pay since the monthly cheque from her trust fund wasn't due for another two weeks.

"Babe," he said, taking her to one side at a party he was hosting, "I likes you a lot and I really would like to help because I know you gettin' the habit. But I don' give credit an' I don' know any dealer who does. Let's come to some kind of an arrangement."

"What arrangement?"

"Well now, you owes me a hun'red bucks so what you prepared to do for a hun'red bucks?"

She didn't catch on at first but then the penny dropped as she stared at him and his eyes widened as they fell to admire her cleavage.

"Oh no," she said. "I'm not selling myself for drugs money. I can wait the two weeks and I'll come back and see you."

She left the party and Lucius thought: Yeah, babe, you goin' last two whole weeks? I'll give you forty eight hours a'fore you come knockin' at my door else I cut off my own jimbob an' fry it on the hob for a san'ich. And he went to his bed smiling and then laughing as he screwed the fine fox who was hanging on to him.

He had seen it all before and thus, Lucius knew he was right when he gave her forty eight hours because she was back two nights later, not looking bad but not looking good. She had been on the stuff for six whole months and she was hooked and her withdrawal symptoms were giving her anxiety and deep depression, shakes and sweating.

She had again borrowed money from her Aunt Emilia and Lucius him two hundred dollars for the powder he gave her but it was really three hundred dollars worth. For the other hundred dollars, she sat on his black snake for thirty minutes, gyrating her hips and jiggling her tits in his face – and then he really started to concentrate on her. She stayed the night and they screwed again before she left the next morning.

And thus the relationship continued. The more time

went on, the more she became hooked – but she wasn't greedy; she controlled her habit as much as she could and when she didn't have sufficient funds to finance the habit, she either had sex with him or he allowed his friends (but only close friends) to do the job and one party evening, he invited some classy pieces of ass to his very private party and he saw much potential here and it very soon developed into a nice little side-line for him. The foxes remained in his employ for as long as he could use them. And Susanne-Marie went along quite willingly.

****

All good things must inevitably come to an end and the relationship between Lucius and Susanne-Marie was always going to be doomed to an ignominious end. The relationship was good while it lasted but her relationships always fizzled out for one reason or another.

They were eating in a side street restaurant in Manhattan's East Side. The food was good and the wine and conversation flowed freely. They were making plans about this and that and talking about him and her and a nondescript sedan pulled up outside the restaurant and three men got out. They walked calmly into the restaurant where two stood by the door and away from the table and ready to open it for a quick getaway while the other pulled a silenced pistol and put three bullets into Lucius' head.

It later transpired that Lucius had been fallen foul of the Chinese gangs who were springing up in the city, he was cheating them out of a large portion of their money and they didn't appreciate being cheated. Thus, they sent an assassin to deliver their message. They left Susanne-Marie sitting at the table and screaming. It could have been because of the shock of the assassination or it simply could have been that her supply of good skag had suddenly been cut off.

After being interviewed by the police, she returned

to Lucius' apartment where she took a large quantity of half cut heroin and money from his safe (a considerable amount of money and which she deposited in her checking account) and fled the nest. There was nothing for her here; she didn't want to spend the rest of her life dealing drugs or running call girls. All of that was in a man's world; she wanted her own world and had no intention of ending up like Lucius. Lucius was past news, a past experience, but her future was misty and she couldn't see it.

Thus, she slowly drifted towards an uncertain future.

****

In the few years leading up to the summer idyll of 1967, she had drifted from one job to another, one boyfriend to another (Lucius had been one of them) and one apartment to another. Her schoolfriends had disappeared out of sight as soon as she had made her way to Brooklyn and those people she knew were either from wherever she worked or from the local neighborhood where she had flopped down for however long. Yet she still remembered Jeff Klein who had gone to Vietnam with the army and she mourned him occasionally, even though she didn't know of his fate.

She drifted away from Emilia and Tony (who had no children of their own) and cultivated people her own age. They would understand her better, would share what they had, stand her a few bucks occasionally (the stolen money from Lucius was gradually soaking away) – and she always paid back. She was no hustler but she had survived thus far to tell the tale to anyone who wanted to listen.

She always had money because when the trust fund stopped sending her monthly cheques, she had Lucius to rely on, and what she had left from Lucius' safe was going to keep her for a while yet.

The descent into prostitution, even though it was

only for Lucius and his chosen friends, was as easy as it had been slipping into the drugs culture of New York but there was always enough money to have a good time, to entertain, to be entertained, to buy drugs so she could go off to another world where her problems didn't exist. And this is what she did occasionally to raise money. Why, she thought, should I put a dent into my checking account? That's a gift from Lucius and only for special occasions – and maybe for when I'm stony broke.

And she discovered that the easier the route to dreamland became, the more she embraced it.

****

Yes, in the few years before she embraced the summer of love, she quickly fell into a deeper drugs habit with punks, scum and the general detritus of human life in the darker parts of Brooklyn but when she heard through an obscure grapevine that a big gathering was about to take place in Monterey on the west coast, she abandoned Brooklyn to its degradation and moved west to Southern California by hitching a lift in a hippy automobile, the owner of which she knew reasonably well and who happened to be going in the same direction.

They lived the couple of weeks together, shared their dope, told their tales and sung their songs of love and getting high and then split in August when they came to Haight Ashbury. And although San Francisco and later Woodstock had fuelled her destructive love and drugs habit, her decline into drink, drugs and human degradation was gradual, in that it took years before she finally saw the darkness of her vile soul.

By the time Monterey came around in June of 1967, Susanne-Marie was embracing everything the Summer of Love in the Haight Ashbury district of San Francisco had to offer, along with all the other hippies, draft dodgers and various human detritus. But Susanne-Marie took the Volume 1 Issue 5 of the *San Francisco Oracle's* article of the big event literally:

> *A new concept of celebrations beneath the human underground must emerge, become conscious, and be shared, so a revolution can be formed with a renaissance of compassion, awareness, and love, and the revelation of unity for all mankind.*

She became conscious of this new concept, and embraced the idea of compassion, awareness and free love and alongside it went a copious amount of drugs of all sorts which she welcomed like she would a bag of candy.

By the time of Monterey, she was smoking heroin, snorting coke and popping pills to her heart's content. She tried LSD but the effect was frightening to her and she left it alone. This was one drug she only took one shot of and she didn't want to spend any time at all suffering weird nightmares in her hours of wakefulness.

She went to the festival at Monterey in Southern California where she listened and rocked and bopped to Jimmi Hendrix, The Who, Janis Joplin, Otis Redding and there was Eric Burdon and The Animals, Jefferson Airplane, The Byrds and there was Simon and Garfunkel and The Grateful Dead. There was Ravi Shankar, a true master of the sitar and the music of the Indian sub-continent and there was John Phillips with The Mamas and The Papas (Phillips had organised this festival alongside Lou Adler, Alan Pariser and Derek Taylor) and Phillips introduced a young singer by the name of Scott McKenzie who sang about San Francisco and having flowers in your hair.

She tagged along with Jess Remington, eight years her junior and a college drop out. She had flowers in her hair and heaven seemed to be around every corner. She spent a lot of her money on Jess but he didn't reciprocate. She loaned him five hundred dollars because he wanted to buy a fabulous guitar he had seen in a music store and she never saw him again. He was a taker and never a giver and by the time she found that out, Jess was long gone, lost somewhere in the hazy culture of San Francisco and singing his self-composed folk songs on his new guitar, and then in despair and when she got bored with Haight Ashbury, she drifted south to Los Angeles.

She ran into a group of hippies one day who said they had a commune somewhere in Death Valley National Park. She had nothing else to do, nowhere to go and no one to go to nowhere with, so she hooked herself on to them and went along to be introduced to the commune.

Life at the commune was weird and it was run by this self-proclaimed Messiah-like creature who always had a weird and staring look in his eyes and the unkempt hair and beard made him look like Rasputin. It seemed he had total control over the commune and everyone in it. What he said had to be done was done. What he said was going to happen, they made it happen on his behalf and although he had never done her any personal harm, Susanne-Marie was frightened of him.

They used to take it in turns to go somewhere for supplies but the commune was run on strict rules and the guy who thought he was the Messiah kept a close rein on those whom he thought might try and make a run for it. He slept with most of the chicks and whenever he wanted to because they also saw him as the Messiah.

At some point, they all started talking about Helter Skelter in the context of a race war against the black population in America because they were taking over everything and they needed putting in their place and her passport, identification and money were confiscated and kept on her behalf and Susanne-Marie began to wonder how she had gotten in with this bunch of wackos in the first place. Okay, so she knew she had drifted towards them but this commune was weird out of all proportion.

She, for perhaps the first time in her life, was scared of someone, of some people, and the Messiah guy and several of his female followers were those she was afraid of most of all. They were bordering on insane and going nowhere except on a journey to Hell and they had no intentions of coming back but every intention of taking the commune and its inhabitants with them.

It was time to bring in stores for the commune and today was her lucky day; she was chosen to go with some of the Messiah's closest confidantes, Susan Atkins, Leslie van Houten, Patricia Krenwinkel and Linda Kasabian, to get what was necessary. By incredible luck, she managed to retrieve her passport, identification and what money she immediately could lay her hands on (which turned out to be more than she had been forced to hand over) and went with them into Los Angeles. They went into a supermarket on the edge of the city and Susanne-Marie managed to feign a visit to the ladies rest room, where she effected her escape through the rear fire exit, hailed a cab a few streets away and asked to be taken to the airport. Two hours later, she was on a flight back to New York.

****

She was back in Brooklyn. She rented a cheap apartment because her money was running out and it wasn't long before she started turning tricks to survive. And then in the summer of 1969, history, it seemed, was beginning to repeat itself.

At some point in her slow downward slide, she hooked up with Luis Ramonde, a Mexican illegal immigrant who was bumming around Brooklyn and at some point, he ran into Susanne-Marie. Down and practically out as they were, they liked each other and while she was attracted to his piercing blue eyes, he was attracted to her by the promise of future wealth, although in her drug fueled hazes, she had over time forgotten when she was due to inherit the de Francia estate.

But Luis had the gift of the gab and knew how to talk to people, get favors from them, borrow small amounts of money, drugs, weed, crack, he knew how to steal quarters from phone boxes, steal from stores without getting caught. This guy was streetwise and Susanne-Marie attached to him like a fly to dog mess in the gutter.

When they hooked up together, he had somewhere to live, a base from which he could operate, and she had a sometime supply of whatever skag and other garbage of the drug world Luis had to give her and she turned tricks to keep them fed when the meagre social welfare money ran out. But they enjoyed each others company, roamed the city together, hung out together, comforted each other during the bad times and laughed together during the good times. They both said to each other in these times of deepest depression that soon, the good times would come and they would be here to stay.

****

And then Woodstock happened.

They journeyed north west into New York State to the Catskill Mountains and found a place called Bethel in Sullivan County where the music festival of Woodstock was about to encompass all that was the current trend in rock music and firmly cemented the counter-culture of the youth of the day.

For as far as the eye could see on this Farmer John dairy farm in the solitude of the countryside, there were tens of thousands of hippies, college dropouts, drug users, people who had reached the highest heights, people who sang, acted, floated on their waves of LSD or whatever else they were getting high on or just placed themselves among the thronging tens and hundreds of thousands and spread their words of peace and love.

And when the music came, it was heavenly bliss. Ravi Shankar made another appearance, as did The Grateful Dead, Janis Joplin and Jimmi Hendrix. There was Arlo Guthrie, Joan Baez and Santana. There was Creedence Clearwater Revival and there was The Who and Joe Cocker.

Everybody rocked and everybody bopped and if they didn't know how to rock or bop, they simply moved to the rhythm of the never ending music, smoked and snorted their dope, took their LSD and their uppers and downers and in betweeners, got high, got low, got spaced out and drank their cans of coke or beer and Heaven was everywhere they touched. They skinny dipped in the pool behind the stage and they reveled in the New York summer sunshine (sometimes, it rained over the weekend but that didn't bother them) and this was even better than Monterey and it was never going to end.

But it did end. After three days, Woodstock began to wind down and everybody who had a home to go to drifted towards home; if they didn't have a home to go to, well, they simply drifted away or drove away in their hippie automobiles and simply got swallowed up in time and space.

Life got back to normal in Brooklyn where Luis and Susanne-Marie got on with their daily lives and they were happy while the weather was still warm.

As the colder weather loomed, they both hustled on the streets to try and increase their supply of dope – whatever they could get – and they managed to stay low on the stuff for as long as possible. Hustling on the streets of New York in the dead of winter was for losers but Luis and Susanne-Marie planned to live in the apartment through the winter and go out as little as possible (maybe in the daytime though because hustling wasn't so bad then; there were more people on the streets, there was so much more going on and nobody really noticed you if you kept your head down and did quiet business).

Luis mentioned he had heard of a rock concert out west which was due to start around December time but Susanne-Marie said she was tired of travelling to rock concerts and she didn't want to go way out west to Altamont in California to see The Rolling Stones.

When December came and the snow and ice and freezing northerly winds came with it, the plan they had embraced during the warm summer months hadn't quite worked out the way they wanted. They were still trying to buy dope but for some reason, it was in short supply and what was available had been cut so many times, it didn't do the job it was supposed to do but it still cost whatever the going rate was for uncut skag.

No point in saying this wasn't fair. Who you gonna complain to, my man? Fuckin' tradin' stann'ards officer? He prob'ly at the end of the queue so shut your whinin' and pay up if you want some or get the fuck outta here.

December was then a miserable and depressing month for Luis and Susanne-Marie. Luis knew how to score when times and the supply were hard and he saved some for his girl – but not much. As times became harder, her cut was less and less and it was never fifty fifty like Luis had promised her. Yes, he gave but he was more of a taker than a giver and so long as she never found out, well, he was going to be okay. After all, skag was skag and like a stiff dick, nothing compensated for it.

He never believed that bullshit about her coming into money. How many times had he heard that from some punk who wanted to borrow a few bucks to score from the man?

But he loved her. In his crazy, mixed up world, he loved her. He would do anything for her (except cut his skag fifty fifty with her – that was purely a guy thing) and he genuinely felt pangs of guilt when she was so sick she couldn't move and she had bad headaches and sweat was pouring from her because she was going through horrendous withdrawal symptoms.

Things got worse one day when all of her bad memories of recent years came back. One day, just before the Christmas holiday, she received mail in the post from Emilia and Tony to say her mother had died in the asylum. The authorities applied to the trustees of her estate for funds to give her a decent burial, which they did, but Susanne-Marie was too sick to attend. She simply managed to get herself out of the apartment and on to the street to buy cigarettes, pain killers and a newspaper. Emilia and Tony attended the funeral on her behalf and eventually, over a short period of time, they lost complete touch with Susanne-Marie.

When she returned to the apartment she sat down and swallowed a handful of the pain killers. At least they worked part of the way and might even last until she got more dope from Luis. She read the newspaper and the main article was about a guy called Charles Manson and some of his followers being charged with the murders of the Sharon Tate household and other killings. She put the paper down and went into the bathroom. She threw up in the toilet and started to shake and sweat and it was never like this when she had no dope – this was worse because she was frightened; frightened at how close she had come to either being killed or being involved in the killings. The four women she knew, those from whom she had escaped on her last shopping trip with them in Los Angeles, had all been named in the killings and were now under arrest waiting trial.

The guy named Charles Manson was the Messiah she

had always been afraid of at the commune and she thanked her good fortune for deciding on the spur of the moment that morning when she had retrieved her passport, money and identification to cut and run as fast and as far away as she possibly could.

She wept, from fear and finally relief that she was here in New York and not rotting in some hidden grave in Death Valley or some prison cell in Los Angeles County awaiting trial for multiple and brutal murder.

Luis came home and when she told him about the west coast, he comforted her as best he could and they both took a shot of good stuff and got high as kites and life was good to them and somehow, they managed to survive yet another winter in New York.

****

All good things come to an end. It is the nature of things within God's creation that anything which is good has an equal and opposite side and that side is called bad or evil. They had graduated from Brooklyn to South Bronx when the man came looking for the rent and they hadn't got it (well, they had but what they had would buy some good skag and anyway, South Bronx wasn't any worse than the seedier side of the Brooklyn they had graduated to).

It was bad what happened to Luis on Christmas Eve 1972 and it was the evil within the perpetrators that made sure he wasn't going to survive.

He was out on the streets and the snow was blowing in his face and the ice cold wind from the north was freezing his teeth and his cheeks and lips and this wasn't the weather for hustling, but he got lucky and scored a good amount and started to make his way towards the all night café on the corner of East 157th and Elton Avenue and when he arrived, he tapped the window and Susanne-Marie, dark circles around her eyes, looked up and smiled at him when he gave her the thumbs up to signify he had scored good.

He hadn't noticed the three punks who had been following him since he had made the trade and waiting for an opportune moment in which to take what he had. And then the knife went in his back and he slid down the window, trying to hang on to the shiny glass, and blood was pouring from his mouth and the deep wound in his back and Susanne-Marie didn't at first comprehend what was happening and the hoodlums were desperately searching his clothes for the skag but they couldn't find it and Susanne-Marie screamed as she saw his blood pouring down the window of the café and she saw him sink slowly to the sidewalk. She ran out and the hoodlums ran towards Third Avenue and disappeared into the snow and mist and icy winds of the night.

She had to think fast before the cops came. She searched his pockets but there was nothing. She removed the contents of his money belt, which was all of two hundred dollars, and then thought hard for a few seconds. Then the light suddenly came on in her head and she put her right hand down the back of his pants and retrieved the skag. He always said: If I hide it in the ass of my jockeys, it gets warm and when you get a taste, babe, you are kissing my ass. She always laughed at that but she wasn't laughing now.

Before anyone noticed, she shoved it and the money down her cleavage (there was plenty of room there to hide stuff) and waited. Someone had called the police and she could hear a siren coming closer. There was a cop car and an ambulance following. By the time they reached him, Luis was dead and Susanne-Marie wept.

She went to the hospital and then to the precinct where she gave her statement to the police and they gave her a ride home in the neighborhood car. They dropped her at the entrance to her apartment.

She had planned for Christmas Eve to be so different than those gone before. She was going to tell Luis that she was expecting their first child and she wanted them to be together for ever and a day and maybe they could get married so the child could be brought up knowing both parents. But some thug with a switch blade had ended all of her plans and the night had ended in blood and murder and the shattering of the only dream she had left.

She spent Christmas Day and the next day junked up to the eyeballs and hoped that when she started to come out of it, she might begin to be able to forget Luis. Luis had been fun. He had been a good lover, a good companion, a good laugh when she was down. And when he was down, it wasn't often and anyway, he soon managed to climb himself out of it.

There was no money for a decent burial so the local authority cremated him and gave Susanne-Marie the ashes. One day, for some reason unknown to her, the ashes became mislaid. In her drug-fueled and drunken state of mind, she had no time to care what had happened to the ashes.

But from that point on, Christmas Eve 1972, she began her decline into drink and drugs and did so with a passion which knew no bounds.

****

The baby, a girl, was born July 10th 1973 and by that time, Susanne-Marie was so utterly soaked in drink and drugs, it was felt that she was incapable of bringing up the child and thus, her nearest family (Emilia and Tony Romano) were given sole custody of two month old Susie. She had an infinitely better chance with them in Brooklyn Heights than she would have had with Susanne-Marie in the darkest depths of South Bronx and its collection of drug addicts, dime whores, thieves, killers, pimps and the rest of the Borough's human trash.

The decline into a long term haze of drink and drugs was slow at first but when the momentum began to gather pace, she really put her heart and soul into it. She stopped going to see her aunt in Brooklyn Heights because (A) Emilia had told her never to come to her house drugged or drunk up to the eyeballs or in possession of drugs or drink and (B) never to bring any waste of space boyfriend to her house or any other downbeat acquaintances she had. When she cleaned herself up, she was welcome, but not until, and if she wanted to argue about her access rights to Susie, she must go and see an attorney and fight it in court.

Susanne-Marie didn't have the money for an attorney. She didn't even have the money to buy food for the next day and so she had to comply with Emilia's ruling (after bumming fifty dollars from her).

Fuck her, she thought. Who does she think she is? I'm better than her. I screw better than her and I got more money than her. Or I will have and then we'll see who's better than who, ya fuckin' douchebag bitch.

Now she was even thinking drugged up and drunk South Bronx talk, rapidly picking up the patois of the city streets. It was a far cry from snooty New Rochelle, buried in the heart of Westchester. It was like an evil spirit taking control of her. There was nothing she could do about it and, it seemed, there was nothing she wanted to do about it.

But thinking about her circumstances, it seemed history was repeating itself. She had lost her child, her first born and her mother had lost her first child too, and Susanne-Marie wondered if an abortion counted. She thought maybe it did because even at two months, her mother must have become attached to the child and perhaps planned for its future.

****

She soon forgot the baby but somewhere within her blown to bits mind, she was aware there was someone else in her life but she couldn't remember who it was. She knew there had been a long term boyfriend but she had even forgotten his name. It bugged her betimes and she drank to try and remember who it was but there was nothing which was brought to her mind. Her brain was addled with drink and drugs (whatever she could get with the money she had) and she remembered precious little now. Sometimes, she would wake in the night crying out Luis' name and sometimes, it would be Susie's name and sometimes, it would be Jeff Klein's name, but she would lay back down to sleep after taking a slug of whiskey or smoking some skag (if she had it) or just a few ordinary cigarettes and disappear once more into the oblivion of her nightmare world of sleep.

****

The tenement building was condemned by the Bronx Borough authorities but she ignored the notice: it was too complicated for her to understand. Damn, but she had quite forgotten how old she even was (this was 1975 and she was thirty-six years of age). But that didn't matter. She had no time to worry about her age: she had more important things to worry about such as where the next supply of drink and drugs was coming from. She didn't even have a couple of bucks to buy a pack of cigarettes.

She was a God-awful mess. She rarely took a shower these days and couldn't even remember the last time she had climbed into a bath of hot, soapy water. Her meals were irregular and she only ate when she had something in the kitchen cupboard to eat (the refrigerator hadn't been working in months) but food took second place (sometimes third place) to everything else and her weight began to drop dramatically. Her priorities for human survival were not correct by any stretch of the imagination but she knew what was important – a supply of skag or pills or whatever she could get her hands on, plenty of drink, even if it was illegally distilled, and someone who would pay to screw her so she could get money to buy the things which were important to her. It was like a never ending carousel.

She sold herself in flophouses for dollars and dimes to anyone who wanted the soiled goods and to anyone who could stomach the smell of her. She was beginning to lose her teeth and she thought how her spider's smile used to work on so many of the guys back home and now the locals called her Dirty Susy because she never washed (when she was going out, she might throw water on her makeup-caked face or she might go to the trouble of having a shower if the system was working) but they tolerated her because for the most part, the degradation of this section of humankind was rarely any better than what she was and anyway, she had the biggest tits around and she could get anyone she wanted.

****

She was riddled with primary and secondary syphilis and by the time the team of Borough officials came to move her out of her condemned tenement building, she could barely walk without feeling excruciating pain from the infected papules and nodules which covered her body. It was no business of theirs: they were here to effect an eviction and they had a job to do. Where she went to after this was the problem of the welfare people or housing or whoever gave a damn.

She roamed the icy cold windswept streets of a November South Bronx in search of whatever might make her happy. She had no home to go to or anywhere she could call home and her brain and thought patterns were so addled with the intake of drink and drugs and the destructive syphilitic disease, she didn't know where she was or what she was doing. She had an idea she had an aunt who lived in Brooklyn Heights but she didn't know in which direction it was or how far away it was (it was fourteen miles south but for all she knew at that moment in her life, it could have been the dark side of the moon).

But she had nowhere else to go and if only she could remember the address. Never mind, she could ask someone when she got to Brooklyn. And so she started walking and the icy wind howled and the thin coat she had around her was grossly insufficient at keeping out the cold and thus, she huddled herself together and slowly scraped along the sidewalk in the direction she thought she ought to go.

She stopped dozens of times to shelter in store doorways or if some homeless group had a fire going on an abandoned lot, she would warm herself and she took a few sips of warm soup or coffee when one of these groups offered it.

She fell a number of times, scraping her hands and banging her head on the sidewalk and it was a struggle to get up and start walking again but somehow, she managed to do it and she knew she was almost there when she saw a bright light in the distance and it grew steadily in size and she just knew she was almost where she wanted to be. All she had to do was ask someone where Emilia and Tony lived but people ignored her and walked quickly by her.

She began to ignore the stares and the people stepping away from her because most of her vision was now taken up by the light which was now not so distant. It was getting closer and closer and something in the deep of her tortured mind told her this was her salvation and she must go on until she reached it. But she had been walking for hours, perhaps days (who knows?) and she didn't know where in the world she even was – or even *when* she was.

****

She woke up in a hospital bed at Bronx Lebanon and she didn't know where she was until a nurse told her. She was in and out of consciousness often and was given occasional sips of water when she was awake. A drip was feeding her medication to try and fight her hopelessly spreading syphilis and the general prognosis was that she wouldn't last through the night. She was heavily under the influence of hard drugs, her liver was all but shot to pieces because of the heavy intake of alcohol, she was desperately undernourished and she was hypothermic because of walking the endless streets in the cold winds of November.

She breathed her last the following evening and her last conscious thought took her back to the night of the Graduation Ball and this time, it was different. Jeff Klein was making passionate love to her and she was in Heaven as she felt him go deep inside her and she cried out for him never to stop and how she would always love him and…

And her entire system slowly collapsed inward and finally shut down and she closed her eyes in death.

****

Who was there to mourn her passing, save for a sad looking padre who hadn't even known her at her worse moments in her recent life, a few officials and Emilia and Tony Romano. Little Susie was not present because they would not permit a child so young and impressionable to attend a funeral. She hardly knew her mother anyway and certainly not enough to call her mama and thus, Emilia and Tony decided it was not the best place for a young and innocent soul such as she.

The rain poured persistently at the funeral and it seemed that today, it was going to rain for ever.

Mockingbird Heights: June 2008

It is said that Mockingbird Heights was so named because John Saville Weston II swore he heard a mockingbird sing in the woods surrounding the fields and forests he owned and farmed. It was unusual because prior to the second half of the nineteenth century, the mockingbird was never seen or heard north of New Jersey. Thus, to keep the memory alive, and vibrant, he built a grand and palatial home for himself and his wife. He named it Mockingbird Heights. Two sons, John and Jethro came in 1860 and 1870 respectively.

The parties and celebrations, the weddings and christenings it saw over the years were legendary: the Christmas and New Year festivities were a sight to behold. The birthdays, the coming home of his sons from boarding school and university, were occasions full of the joy every home should have.

John Saville Weston II prospered and raised the very finest dairy herd of Jersey and Guernsey cattle and the fat dairy herds roamed the lush and green acres, gorged on the high quality grass and produced milk, cream, butter and cheese to die for. His forested acres of maple trees annually yielded the very finest quality maple syrup and his hives of bees guaranteed a sizeable income on an annual basis.

And thus at the close of the century, Mockingbird Heights resided atop the hill overlooking the rich farmland of Rutland County, at peace with the world and as solid as the day the building was first occupied.

In 1890, John Saville Weston II passed on from this life and all of his property and wealth passed on to his two sons, John Saville Weston III and Jethro Saville Weston, both having equal shares in the estate. They were the sole beneficiaries of his last will and testament and when Jethro was fatally wounded in the year 1900 during the Philippine

/ American War, his own wealth and his share in the farm, because he died without issue, passed to his brother John, who was now the last male member of his line.

John Saville Weston III married Susanne-Marie Trelawney in April of 1885 and ten years later, she gave birth to their only child, Pandora Lillian. Susanne-Marie died in childbirth.

****

The de Francia family had come to prominence in the Mexican Revolution by backing and arming the revolutionaries Pancho Villa and Emeliano Zapata. Zapata was assassinated in April 1919 under the auspices of the government of Venustiano Carranza and Pancho Villa was assassinated in Parral in the Province of Chihuahua on the orders of President Avaro Obregon.

After the assassination of their last ally, Jorge de Francia took his ill gotten gains, his wife, his son Tomas and his daughter Emilia and escaped across the Rio Grande into El Paso, Texas. From El Paso, they travelled nearly twenty five hundred miles across the United States of America to be as far away as possible from the hotbed of revolution and eventually settled in Vermont.

But in the general scheme of things, in the history of the Saul - de Francia family, Jorge and his wife never figured much and were deemed never that important to be noticed. They settled with their money, invested it wisely and later invested a good deal of it (extremely profitably) in arming the forces fighting against Generalissimo Franco in Spain. It seemed they were fated to be involved in one revolution after another and had a penchant for selling illicit arms.

But the de Francia family, over the years between the marriages of their son Tomas and daughter Emilia and the end of the Korean War, faded slowly from view. Athenia,

Pandora's child, and her husband, Tomas de Francia, visited on rare occasions but it was more Tomas keeping in touch with his family roots than he and Athenia together being sociable and embracing family.

Jorge had prospered greatly from the Spanish Civil War but when he tried to negotiate an arms deal with Fidel Castro's Communist bandits, who were fighting Fulgencio Batista, the President of Cuba, in his almost fratricidal civil war, he was quietly spoken to by federal agents and told not to become involved any further. Castro was being armed by the Russians and Batista, they suspected, was not going to win. Jorge de Francia was duly informed that it was none of his business and he should not attempt to sell illegal arms to the island of Cuba.

But ever eager for financial gain from revolution, and because of the sense of adventure it gave him, almost from the moment he settled with his family in Vermont, he supplied illicit arms to governments and rebel forces in Central and South America where violent revolution was almost a daily occurrence. One of his major successes was providing arms for the government forces of President Eusebio Ayala in his three year war with Bolivia over ownership of the Gran Chaco region (supposedly rich in oil) which ended in 1935 and a resounding victory for Paraguay. Jorge later travelled to the city of Ascunsion to receive the personal gratitude of the President himself.

By 1961, at the time he was being investigated by federal agents for his activities in Central and South America, Jorge de Francia contracted lung cancer and passed on from this life on the day President Kennedy and Nikita Krushchev agreed to a mutual withdrawal from the island republic of Cuba. His wife succeeded him by four years, she dying of a demential disease in a nursing home.

****

Pandora Lillian Weston was married to Reverend Ethan Saul, a firebrand Baptist preacher, in 1918 and gave birth to her only daughter, Athenia, in October 1920.

On Harvest Festival Sunday in October of 1938, Ethan Saul raped his own daughter after he found her canoodling with a boyfriend in the barn of the farm when they both should have been at the church service.

The result of the rape was aborted two months later under the direct instructions of her mother and Athenia forever secretly mourned the loss of her child. But there was another child after Tomas and Athenia married. She was Susanne-Marie, born at four in the morning of Friday November 3 1939 and she was named after her maternal great grandmother.

The marriage was not a happy one and as she and Tomas simply existed together but drifted ever further apart, he began to get his sexual kicks elsewhere, but when he raped Susanne-Marie, his own daughter, Pandora knifed him to death after telling him she herself had been raped by her own father.

She escaped the electric chair by reasons of insanity but she was committed to serve a life sentence in an asylum. After twelve years in the asylum, rather than face the rest of her life among mad people, she took her own life by hording her medication for a month and then taking a massive overdose.

Four years after giving birth to her only child, Susie, Susanne-Marie de Francia, being a hopeless alcoholic and drug addict and riddled with syphilis, passed on from this life in November of 1976. Susie had been taken into care four years previous to her mother's death by her great aunt, Emilia de Francia Romano and her husband Anthony Romano but on Susanne-Marie's death, Susie inherited what was left of the estate – and it still remained a considerable amount of property and investments. The estate included Mockingbird Heights and its surrounding forest and farmland and all was kept in trust for her.

****

That is the history and the gradual decline over the years of Mockingbird Heights, the Saul – de Francia family and all of its clan members, their achievements and their successes: there were no failures I could find up to the time when Pandora Lillian married Reverend Ethan Saul. But there is an opposing force. If you believe in Isaac Newton's Third Law of Motion, which goes something like: when one body exerts a force on a second body, the second body simultaneously exerts a force equal in magnitude and opposite in direction on the first body (yes, I know it applies to the physics of mechanics, but this is an existential allegory – I think that is what you call it, but you know what I mean) then you will believe in the opposing forces of nature, be it human or otherwise. The fault may have lain with Pandora's father, John Weston III, who was vehement in his wish that she should not marry Lucas Richmond but Ethan Saul instead. Who knows precisely when the rot started to set in?

****

And how do I know the history of this family? Well, Pandora kept diaries and her daughter, Athenia, kept diaries; Susanne-Marie, Athenia's daughter, kept diaries (up to a point) and Pandora's great granddaughter, Susie, kept diaries, which included a comprehensive history of all the family members; so when I launched my own investigations, the workload was not as heavy as I first suspected it would be.

All kept very prolific diaries and when Susie launched herself from the roof of my fifty floor apartment building in Manhattan, all of those diaries came into my possession: because do you know what? Susie was without issue also, no family whatsoever, and totally unbeknown to me, she left me everything in her last will and testament.

It came as an utter shock to me and she never once indicated to me that she had done this; not once ever in our three year relationship. The estate ran into millions of dollars and cold-hearted son of a bitch that I am (at least according to Anna, my ex-wife) I never kept a solitary cent – except for the diaries which were actually of no use to anyone at all and of no monetary value.

The diaries make superlatively interesting reading but the salient points of their escapades, their dirty dealings, the drunkenness, the suicides, the insanity – and there is more than one murder to my knowledge – make the most interesting reading. Well, that's a rap on twentieth century social behaviour! And it all seemed to centre on Mockingbird Heights and its generations of misfits, criminals and womanisers, its drug addicts and alcoholics.

Now there is an idea! Maybe ghosts, evil spirits, call them what you will, are those spirits who for some reason cannot gain entry to Heaven or Hell and gather somewhere while waiting for a celestial decision on where they will spend the rest of eternity. Just picking at straws while I suck on the end of my finger. But an interesting hypothesis nonetheless.

But Susie once told me about her family in a postage stamp size history (before I read the full account). I guess she felt I had to know. I don't think she told me as a warning before I committed myself to a relationship; rather, it simply seemed like a general point of conversation.

****

Not too long after Susie took her leap of faith, I discovered the true extent of her wealth when her attorneys told me she had left me everything. I mean, apart from her house on

Staten Island, her investments, her several private pension plans (her life insurances were invalid because of her suicide) there was the palatial, although very much run down house in Vermont (Mockingbird Heights) and the rich arable land surrounding it, plus the forest of maple trees.

After my one and only visit, I tried to sell it off but there were no takers and this was hardly surprising considering the state of the place and what lived there. A few said the place felt 'haunted' and gave them the creeps. The herd of Guernsey and Jersey cattle were long since gone and the maples in the forest were either diseased or choking with stinging nettles or brambles and other creeping plants. The hives of bees had long since disappeared and the entire tract of what was once the arable farmland of Mockingbird Heights looked dead and sterile. So I just left it at that. Perhaps someone would buy the land for development (or farming) and demolish the old house. It does not and cannot matter to me now.

****

Somewhere along a country lane on Route 100 just out of Killington, a derelict house by the name of Mockingbird Heights sits atop a flattened hill. Why am I drawn to this place when I have no true ownership interest in it? I knew the value of the surrounding land, albeit overgrown but still extremely valuable development land, and I knew the total value of Susie's financial worth but I didn't want to profit from her death so I asked her attorneys if they would take her wealth off my hands and invest it in a children's trust or some other worthy children's charitable cause. They did so.

Nevertheless I had to see inside Mockingbird Heights. It was a curiosity I could not resist. I felt compelled to see it.

But the house; it looked so lonely, so decrepit and abandoned. No one had lived there since the beginning of the war in Korea and when I saw how abandoned it was, I thought of Edgar Allen Poe and his tales of troubled and haunted houses: perhaps even the Marsten House in Stephen King's creepy novel *Salem's Lot* or even a Shirley Jackson creation, *The Haunting of Hill House* (...whatever walks there walks alone...). But I later found that nothing walked alone in that house.

As I stood a few yards from the main entrance, my imagination was running wild: should I go in or not? Even this up close and personal, it looked ghostly and most definitely uninviting.

And random thoughts kept going through my head. What is the atmosphere like? How long has it been like this; I mean, when did the real decay begin to set in? It must once have been so very beautiful but now what does it smell like inside? Musty? Damp? Does it still have furniture? Does it have a basement? What lives in the basement? What is the structure of the house like? I mean the actual structure – the brickwork, the supporting beams, the floors?

I could imagine the smell and decay and dank corridors and the claustrophobic atmosphere of the basement. Wallpaper peeling off, fine plaster dust floating aimlessly in the air and dusting the creaking floorboards. Creaking stair risers. The cloying smell of corruption and age.

I entered and it was as I imagined it to be. I soon began to get shivery feelings, almost as if someone was present in the room. But no, there were only shadows, indistinct and ethereal. But what tangible form does an atmosphere take? Is it a ghost or simply the remains of past thoughts, actions, words said in anger or sadness?

I can almost visualise what it must have been like in its heyday, even though I knew something of its history and it was not so very long ago when Mockingbird Heights was a beautiful and palatial home in the rolling green hills of Vermont. Spring was fresh and green, summer was agreeably warm, fall was golden brown with the pleasant aroma of decomposing leaves and winter was cold, deep and white and full of crystal clarity and a sharpness in the air which was biting, making one want to sit in front of a huge log fire with a glass of fine whiskey or brandy for a companion. But whatever the time of year, everything in the surrounding countryside was always so breath-taking and indescribably beautiful – and it all surrounded this once beautiful house.

Once beautiful?

Now the house was old and ugly, gray and dead and its decay was like a creeping carcinoma worming its way through the crumbling and damp-sodden walls. There was something Poe-esque about its entire structure. It looked like something from a Roger Corman movie, *The House of Usher* or the foreboding residence where walked the vengeful spirit of Ligeia. It is full of atmospheres. Yes, atmospheres, dead and crawling aimlessly. There was definitely the atmosphere of the malevolently dark and lonely House of Usher, with its family history of murder and insanity, of debauchery and illicit sex and drunkenness. It was a truly evil place but the atmosphere of evil didn't hit straight away. One had to be inside to experience it and then it came on gradually until one suddenly became aware of its disturbing existence.

Something was there. Something walked within the confines of its decaying corridors. Again, my thoughts began to wander. It lives in the worm-infested and rotting timbers. It lives in the dusty cobwebs which hang from chandeliers and staircases and doors and furniture. It lives within the spiders that infest the cobwebs, the rats that crawl within the walls and roam the darkened rooms. It exists in the deadness of the place and the ethereal mists which sometimes crawl in from the decaying ground outside.

It roams the dim and stale air. It lives in the fine plaster dust carpeting the bare floorboards and the dust motes in the air. It inhabits the stark silence. It *is* the silence, heavy and oppressive. It is something which, though it lives with its kindred kind, is desperately lonely and seeks contact between two worlds, one real and one ethereal. I know this to be true because I have felt its presence.

I thought: a single match to all of this and it would explode in flames.

I had to keep looking over my shoulder to see if anything was there, something which was trying to reach out and touch me, touch human flesh instead of indistinct nothingness.

I didn't think it was a ghost but only because (at least up until that time) I didn't believe in such things. It is an atmosphere in the real sense of the word. Something left behind, something bad and unacceptable. Yes, some very bad things happened here and the memory of those experiences prevails. It is like when you walk into a room and there are two people who have had a heated argument and they are 'not speaking'. There is an atmosphere because you can feel it. It is very distinct and it is so real, you can take a knife and almost cut it right down the middle and see the two separated halves. You feel as if you want to say something like, "Nice weather for the time of year," – just to try and break the ice, but you know it is useless because what exists is too powerful and overwhelming for you to break down into all of its rational components.

Everywhere I walked in the house there was the musty smell of age-old dampness, mixed with the dust stirred by the sluggish and stale air. Everywhere I walked in the house, the echoes of my footfalls seemed to echo into – nowhere and nowhen.

I am not all that certain of what comprises the

atmosphere in Mockingbird Heights. I know Ethan Saul is a part of it: he must have found his way back somehow. But it is also many other things and people long since (and recently) departed. It is a collection of feelings, emotions, leftovers, of the things that went on here and in other lives through the years when it was alive and functioning as a home (albeit towards the end an unhappy one). But the spirits brought their unhappiness with them and it all adds to the stink of the corruption of this house. Yes, everything that happened to this family over the years and happened here or elsewhere has returned, like an evil magnet attracting its own kind of venality and debasement.

No one or nothing human lives here, of that I can assure you. Whatever exists here is ethereal and most definitely does not walk alone because they are all here, I suspect, all of the Saul – de Francia clan because this is the place they know best of all, this dank and dark passageway to Hell in all its glory. I think thus: pull the house down, yes, because it has fallen into rotten decay, but in Hell, anything is possible and the house will follow them wherever they go in the next world or to wherever their miserable souls are destined to reside.

Ethan Saul is here. I know he is because there is a strong smell of the sour mash whiskey he used to pour down his throat. And Pandora is here also. She once told Ethan to get out and not come back but now the circumstances are different. Now she can't stop him. Perhaps even now in their spirit world, they fight like cat and dog.

There is Jorge de Francia being eternally pursued by the dead who suffered by the arms he sold to the revolutionaries in war torn lands. Nothing much in the diaries ever said anything about his wife, except that she was a wispy little mouse of a thing. But she makes her contribution to the stink in this place, like the rest of them. She must have known and was thus complicit in what Jorge was doing; otherwise, she must have been an incredibly stupid woman not to have been aware of it. At the very least, she lived off the profits of Jorge's illicit dealings.

And there is Athenia – I sense her insane laugh and there is blood on the walls in one of the bedrooms and it was in this room where I felt the strongest presence and I thought I heard a distant scream, as if someone was dying a dreadful death.

And there is Tomas himself, weeping and wailing (I sense this, I hear this somewhere off in the distance of nowhere) because Athenia won't leave him in peace and mayhap he also has to suffer an eternity of that knife going into his stomach and chest and...and other places. No, she will never leave him in peace. Why should she when he raped his own daughter?

And there is Susanne-Marie, the syphilis-ridden and drug and drink fuelled minx who brought so much trouble to the de Francia family in New Rochelle. I could smell her and her diseases and her dirtiness and the stench of her foul body odour.

And, of course, there is Susie. If I'm not one hundred per cent sure of the others (but I think I am) then I am pretty damn certain of Susie. I could never mistake that beautiful scent of Chanel No. 5, only now it is sickeningly cloying and hangs in the sluggishly moving air like a damp mist of cold and icy fog.

But the house, Mockingbird Heights, takes care of them all. Yes, I firmly believe everything that has happened to this family over the years has returned to Mockingbird Heights, like an evil magnet attracting its own kind of evil. Their souls, damned or otherwise, are drawn to this house like flies to dog mess on the sidewalk. This is where they room until, I guess, a place in Hell or elsewhere can be found for them. There is an aura – no, it is more like an afterglow

– which has plagued each generation of this family since I don't know when, and it hangs in the atmosphere of the house. For as long as the house lives, so will the base corruption of its atmosphere and that which exists within it.

Perhaps that is the form ghosts take and all of these dead souls, wherever they resided, have returned to the house to wander its loneliness until its final demise – and perhaps beyond. Who knows? I don't know what the truth of this is. It doesn't matter. All that matters is that it is there and it seems to reach out, trying desperately to reach beyond the confines of the walls, beyond the emptiness of its disintegrating structure to the surrounding hills and woodlands. But it cannot. Its corruption and decay remain confined within the structure of the house and hangs cloyingly in the sluggish air.

I know from delving into the family history that Ethan Saul died by his own hand, a penniless alcoholic, and that Pandora, his wife, spent her final years in an asylum. I know that Athenia murdered her husband because he raped Susanne-Marie (or so it seemed at first) and that she committed suicide rather than face the rest of her life in an asylum. Susanne-Marie gave birth to a daughter, Susie, in 1972 (father Luis Ramonde, a heroin addict and general waste of space) but sank in a revelry of drugs and drink and died of syphilis in a hospital bed in November of 1976.

****

They say the spirits of suicides, insane people, murderers, never find true rest and perhaps the atmosphere is a collective inventory of the decay of their respective intelligences, the evil things they did, the decay of their minds, their amoral corruption and depravity.

I do not believe these things can happen and not leave something behind. Whatever it comprises, I would like to believe it is all that is left of everyone who was in some way connected with this house, even if they are no longer a material part of this world.

Something reached out from beyond life and touched my shoulder. It said my name –"Glen." And there was a faint whiff of perfume.

And then I heard a baby crying and then I heard it laugh. A baby? But was this in truth Athenia's aborted child? Can an aborted two month old foetus laugh? If it indeed can, it was the most evil laugh I have ever heard.

I ran along the corridor and down the creaking stairway at the speed of a top class athlete. I stopped at the open front entrance and looked back. It was late afternoon, but not quite dusk, but the dark at the top of the stairs seemed to be crawling its way down the stairway toward me. I was scared to look for too long into it, scared of what – or who – I might see behind it. It frightened me badly and so I ran like a frightened child from the boogey man.

I know it was Susie who said my name and touched me. I knew it was her because I recognized her voice and the perfume of her Chanel No. 5.

At a distance along the winding trail on the lower slopes of the forested hill on which it stood, I looked one last time at the house and felt relatively safe from the strands of atmosphere reaching out like desperately searching hands to claw me back.

But I thought: No, I'm not going back inside there. But perhaps this family hasn't finished with me yet.

That was and remains a very frightening prospect.

Afterglow: 2008 – 2009

It doesn't take a genius to discover why I had a massive breakdown but four months after Susie took her leap of faith and after I had visited Mockingbird Heights (plus doing more research on her family – reading their diaries etc.), I had a massive breakdown.

It hit me quite suddenly and with the force of a speeding train and by the beginning of February 2009, Anna had taken me back. I guess she felt sorry for me because I couldn't cope with life. She made up a bed for me in the spare bedroom but that only lasted a few weeks and then she took me back into our own bed. There was no sex or any shenanigans like that: I was too drained, both from my experience with Susie and also my colossal breakdown to want there to be another physical side to the renewal of our relationship. But I guess that kind of trust which exists between a 'normal' married couple wasn't quite there with Anna yet. It might have come in time.

She knew nothing of Susie and I never volunteered to tell her until much later, when it was far too late to even consider gaining her trust. Anna never asked me if I had any affairs after she threw me out; she simply assumed that this was the case and that I wouldn't be without a woman for very long. But let me tell you about the presence I felt in my apartment and then I will tell you (eventually, because everything follows in a logical order) of the aftermath.

****

I know what finally tipped me over the edge and plunged me into a black hole of mind-numbing breakdown. For a couple of months, I thought: Is Susie really haunting me, my apartment? I was never one hundred per cent certain until I woke up one morning after having some very bad nightmares in which Susie was the principal character and there it was on the bed; a black velvet choker with a blue tanzanite crystal on a small silver chain. Susie used to wear it – and sometimes, it was the only thing she wore! It jolted me; like a massive electric shock, it jolted me. I threw it in the trash because I didn't want anything of Susie's in my apartment (but the scent of her Chanel No 5 was there with the choker) - and I have to say I don't know from a rational point of view how the choker got there in the first place. Susie must have placed it there but Susie was dead!

But was she? Was she dead? Yes, goddamn it, she was dead because I saw her leap off the roof of my apartment building and I later identified what was left of her body and it was her: I swear it was her.

That smell of her would suddenly appear in the apartment – in the office too! I asked the girls, not very nicely, which of them was wearing Chanel No 5 and every one of the women swore it was not her.

And then one morning, when I was in the men's rest room, I suddenly screamed as I felt the stroke of a whip across my back. It was Susie. She had even followed me into this room where I should at least have some privacy from the female of the species – even from evil spirits, goddamnit!

I recovered, quickly; I had to because I couldn't risk anyone in the office finding out about this. Who was going to believe me anyway?

This kind of thing went on for several weeks and I kept telling her to leave me alone and then I would look up and wonder why everybody was staring at me.

****

Mort Schafer, the Chief Executive Officer (whom I trusted implicitly – but I wasn't going to tell him my secrets regarding Susie), requested my presence in his office one morning.

"Hi, Glen. Sit yourself down. I…er…wanted a very private word with you because you seem to be having some problems lately and I'm here to tell you that if you need any help, I will do all in my power to assist you."

"There's nothing wrong, Mort. I just haven't been sleeping well. I brought this upon myself. What with the divorce and pressure of work and not seeing my kids growing up – I have access rights, but it's not enough. It's too much pressure."

"Yes, but I was waiting for you to tell me because it really isn't any of my business. I didn't want it to appear as if I was interfering in private family matters."

"Well, that is all that is wrong. Really, it is."

"Okay, Glen, let me tell you what I know. One of the guys came in to see me yesterday afternoon – I'm not saying who but he means well – and he said on several occasions, he and others have seen blood seeping through the back of your shirt. And everybody in the office says you mumble to yourself and sometimes you say strange things out loud. Who is Susie? They've also seen you crying."

Just before I was called into his office, I had been in the rest room again and again, Susie (who else and what else could it be?) had lain a ghostly whip across my back and I knew she had fetched blood because I could feel it seeping down my back and down my arm. Mort pointed this out because it was starting to drip on to the carpet in front of his desk.

"Glen, I know this is an unusual request and believe me, there is nothing sinister in this request…but take your shirt off. You are bleeding and I want to know what is happening."

He had caught me out and there was no way I could get out of this so I stood and took my jacket off. The right sleeve of my white shirt was drenched in blood. I took my shirt off and turned my back to him.

There was silence for a few seconds – but it seemed like for ever. And then, "Jesus Christ Almighty, Glen, what are you into? What has been going on here? Which East Side dime whore did this to you? What are you doing to yourself? My God, Glen, you can't come into the office in this state for heaven's sake!"

The bloodied weals came and went and Mort Schafer saw one of them. By the time I would take my shirt off to wash the blood out, the blood would have disappeared, as if it had never been there in the first place. This was weird. Susie obviously had more control over me than I had at first thought. She even had control over how I looked for God's sake!

And then I broke down, in front of him, one of the most powerful men in the Manhattan business world, and he was dumbstruck. He didn't know what to do and quite frankly, I didn't know how to give him guidance on what we should both be doing about this.

Eventually, my tears subsided and he said, "I'm going to call for an ambulance and ask one of the guys in the office to see you to the hospital and he will report back to me. I will swear him to secrecy on pain of losing his job here and anywhere else in Manhattan. But Glen, you have to help me out here. You have to open up to someone because this cannot continue.

"Are you really not okay, Glen? Is there something I should know about, even if it is deeply personal to you? I ask because...well...this is somewhat embarrassing for me but...your colleagues in the office say you keep talking to yourself and it isn't just under your breath. Glen, you have to help me out here because I don't know what's going on. I mean, if this is the start of a nervous breakdown or something like that and you need time away from the office, well, I'll see what I can do to help. But in the meantime, take whatever help the hospital can give you."

"Can you smell Chanel No 5, Mort? Because I can."

"No. no, I can't smell it. Should I b able to? Perhaps that's another symptom of your illness."

But the aroma was receding. Eventually, it was gone.

Jack Ward, one of my chief assistants, came to the hospital in the ambulance with me and by the time we arrived, they had put me in a strait jacket because I was becoming aggressive and violent and I was screaming and yelling for her to get the hell away from me and I must have passed out (did they give me a knock-out sedative?) because the next sensation I was aware of, I woke up in a ward which was securely locked. And I was still in the strait jacket.

****

The six months I was told to take in convalescence seemed all the time in the world I needed and even throughout that time, I sensed Susie's presence. I felt the history of the family held the secret to sending her back to wherever she belonged but I was in no condition to delve any further.

I slowly began to get better: by slowly, I mean by painful inches. I gave up my apartment when Anna took me back because I couldn't go back to it. Not ever. Some guy from a major insurance company took it over and when I asked him a couple of months after he moved in (I returned to pick up some personal belongings I had left behind) if he found anything strange about it, he said no, everything was fine. Neither did I 'smell' Susie while I was there and neither did I feel a 'presence'.

So, Miss Susie had flown the nest from where she had taken her leap of faith. But up to the time I had my breakdown, I suffered her wrath almost every day and night.

Sometimes, it would be a stroke of a cane or whip; at other times, I would simply feel her presence, or smell her perfume or the smoke from one of her cigarillos. Sometimes, she came to me in my dreams and they were always the most horrifying. I can't even begin to describe the horror I felt because they are too upsetting for me.

She was bleeding me dry like a vampire only instead of blood, she was draining me of all human feeling, all emotion, almost everything I ever loved in life. She was gradually wearing me down and there was nothing I could do about it: she was too strong. She taught me the lesson that for me, she was the only one who existed and no one else had the right to any part of me, body or soul.

She would come to me in my dreams at night or suddenly, during the day (and sometimes, as I have already said, at the office) I would suddenly fall asleep, without previously feeling tired or feeling as if I had to sleep, and there she would be, pale and with blood around her lips and I would feel so weak.

Did I say she was bleeding me dry like a vampire? Let me tell you what happened some time after I moved back with Anna. I spent two months in a private sanatorium before Anna took me back: she said the best place for me was back home with the family.

So I moved back with her and stayed well away from other women. I was learning my lesson very quickly.

****

One night, I was in a world of weird dreams and the next thing I knew, Anna was waking me up.

"Hey," she said, "that must have been some dream. You were trying to fight me off."

"I'm sorry – doing things in my sleep again. Must be the medication."

"Don't forget to take it today. I'm taking the kids to school and then I'm going straight on to work so have a relaxing day. There's coffee in the pot but it needs warming. Byeeee!"

And she went. I heard her close the car door and move off down the driveway.

At the very least, I knew I was taking the right medication because Anna vetted everything I was prescribed and she made certain I took it when I was supposed to take it – every last tablet.

I must have fallen into a deep sleep again and this time, the dream was vivid and more than nasty. Susie was in it and she had a mongrel dog by the scruff of its neck and she plunged a huge carving knife into its side and kept slashing away at it, allowing its blood to pour over her. She held the dead animal out to me – "Do you want some, Glen? Do you want some? Do you want some?" – but I refused it and she said, "Kill it, Glen. If you love me, kill it. Kill the goddamn dog and stop being such a cry baby miserable bastard. KILL ITTTTT!!!!"

And then she threw off her dripping with blood peignoir and straddled me and started to make violent love to me and the fucking bitch bit my neck around the carotid artery area.

I suddenly woke and heard myself screaming. I was sweating and it was cold.

I got up and went into the bathroom. When I looked in the mirror, there were two small puncture-like wounds around the carotid arterial area. They were really small, almost insignificant – but I saw them! They were almost like two tiny skin blemishes but they were prominent because I could see them. I felt the area but there was no pain, just a slight numbness around the skin.

I showered, shaved and dressed and went into the kitchen to make coffee. The kitchen door which gave access to the rear garden was open and there were blood stains on the floor; just a few drops, but the sight of the blood jolted me.

I suddenly called out to Doozy, the family Dalmatian (really it was the kids' dog but everybody loved him – they called him Doozy because…well…he was a big flollopy doozy dog and as gentle as gentle could ever be!). "Doozy. Come on, Doozy, it's breakfast time." I could see that Anna had filled his food bowl but it hadn't been touched.

I strolled out into the garden; I didn't particularly want to do it but I felt compelled to do it. I found Doozy behind the greenhouse at the bottom of the garden. He was covered in blood. His throat had been slit from left to right to the extent that his head was almost off and just hung by the neckbone and a carving knife was sticking out of his right side.

I remember sort of screaming or making some gurgling sound of disgust. I remember vomiting at the sight of Doozy lying there. I remember lurching back into the house, into the bathroom to continue vomiting and when I had cleaned myself up, I went into the bedroom and the smell of Chanel No 5 was so overpowering and cloying (this time, it was a smell - a *strong smell* - as opposed to a mild scent). And on the bed was the tanzanite choker. How could that be since I had thrown it in the trash when I still had my apartment?

By the late afternoon, Anna was trying to comfort the kids when Maisie, Jack's wife from next door, brought them back from school. I had been interviewed by the police and the veterinary surgeon had taken Doozy away to be cremated.

I told the cops exactly what I knew; that I woke and

got up around nine and found the kitchen door open. There was no reason for the kitchen door to be open so I walked out to see if I could see anything – and I found Doozy behind the greenhouse. No, I hadn't seen anyone and yes, we get on with our neighbours very well and no, I don't know anyone who has a grudge against us.

At the very back of my mind, I thought this last was a lie but only because of the weird dream I had had about Susie. I didn't tell the cops about the weird dream and neither did I tell Anna. And who was going to believe it had been Susie who killed the dog? Who the hell is Susie, everyone would ask? - and then I would have a whole load of explaining to do and no one would believe it anyway.

I was given further extended sickness leave from my office but after another three months, they offered me very healthy (more than likely because there was no likelihood of me coming back any time soon) severance pay and I took it. Maybe they might have taken a vote of no confidence in me. Who knows? I don't care.

Over the next few months or so, other weird things started to happen and things began to get very scary and I truly believed Susie was responsible from the very beginning. She wanted me and she was going to have me come hell or high water! And something else I reminded myself of – I must stop using clichés in my written and spoken speech.

We didn't get another dog: Doozy was one in a million and couldn't be bettered. And talking about Doozy, something else which turned out to be very weird; there were no fingerprints at all on the knife handle or the blade and it was one of our own kitchen knives. There was no blood on any of my clothes either because I thought at one stage, I might have killed the dog while sleepwalking and while under Susie's influence. I thought that because of the dream, my fingerprints might be on it but the knife was as clean as it could be – apart from the blood. And then I began to question my own assumption that it was Susie who had killed the dog. The prospect of this happening scared the living daylights out of me.

****

What happened over the next three or four months was, given recent circumstances, inevitable. I say inevitable because I really didn't know what to do about this entire affair. What was I supposed to do? Confess all regarding my affair with Susie and how she committed suicide because I spurned her weird interpretation of love? How on earth could I tell Anna that it was Susie who was haunting us (me)? Would she believe me? No. Under the circumstances, I think she would have me permanently committed to an asylum. Well, eventually, she got her wish. But what happened up until that major turning point in my life? Well, since you are sitting on the edge of your seat, I'll tell you.

****

I began to feel a presence, an atmosphere in the house, as if we were being watched and at times, the feeling was quite strong but neither Anna nor the kids ever mentioned it so I had to assume it was just me. I was taking some pretty damn weird medication at the time and I thought how useless it was because all it seemed to be doing was giving me weird experiences and the creeps. But Anna, don't forget, was vetting everything I took.

I had to keep looking over my shoulder to see if anyone was there – but of course, there never was. And sometimes, the feeling was so strong I felt I had to go and hide in a corner.

And then one night in the early summer, I woke and saw Amelia (aged ten years) standing by our bed.

She said, "Daddy, there's a funny lady in my room."

Anna heard her say this and I said to her, "I'll deal with it. She's most likely had a nightmare."

I took Amelia back to her room and there was no one there (except Charlie who slept in the same room). And there was the blue tanzanite pendant. Amelia apparently hadn't noticed this so I picked it up off her bed and put it in the pocket of my dressing gown. I had no intention of telling Anna about this – not yet. There was little point in getting everybody else spooked. I was spooked enough for all of us. What the hell was I going to tell her anyway?

"Was Charlie walking in her sleep?" I asked. "Maybe it was her you saw."

"No, daddy. I saw a weird lady and she frightened me. She was covered in blood. She said it was dog's blood."

"She wasn't real, honey bunch. It was just a bad dream you had and what with us losing Doozy, it's something just playing on your mind. You go back to sleep now but I'll sit with you for a while."

So I sat with her and she soon went back to sleep.

A few weeks later, Joseph (aged twelve years and quite the man of the house the time I was away from Anna) came into our room and woke me. He said, "Dad, I just had a bad dream."

"What was it," I said as I got out of bed to take him back to his room.

"I saw a strange lady walking in the garden. She had Doozy on a lead and a knife was sticking out of his side and his head was hanging to one side. I don't like that lady. Make her go away."

"Joseph, have you been talking with Amelia?"

"About what?"

"About the bad dream she had a couple of weeks ago?"

"No, sir, I haven't. She never told me she had a bad dream."

"Well she did have one but it doesn't matter now."

The feeling of there being a strange and seemingly evil presence in the house gradually began to increase from that point onward and there was nothing I could do to stop it. Anna neither felt nor saw anything and neither did she have weird dreams about a 'funny' lady. There was nothing funny about her if the experience frightened Amelia and Joseph.

I was woken in the early hours a few nights later by Charlie crying in her sleep. I went into her room. Amelia was still asleep and I picked Charlie up out of her bed and I asked her what was wrong and she simply said, "Doozy. Nasty lady. Don't like the nasty lady. Want Doozy back. The nasty lady is hurting him."

So she had had the dream as well. Why was Anna not experiencing this? And then a thought entered my head from nowhere at all: Because she is not an integral part of the equation. Not yet anyway. She only took me back because she felt somehow responsible for me. She only took me back because she felt sort of sorry for me: it didn't necessarily mean to say she loved me and suddenly everything was forgiven, but it seemed a feasible answer to an awkward question.

Not an integral part of the equation? Where the hell did that come from?

Nothing for a week and then all of a sudden, the flowers in the herbaceous border started to wilt and die. They should have gone on for at least another couple of months but their demise and death was quite sudden. Anna and I diligently fed and watered them (I did most of the gardening because I wasn't at work) and the summer wasn't particularly hot or cold so there was no rational reason for it to happen. Then we had a plague – and I mean a plague! – of ants and other creepy crawlies and this went on for around two weeks.

This feeling of there being a presence in the house was getting stronger by the day and I wondered if I should call in a priest to exorcise the damn place but Anna would think I was crazy, that it's me and the medication I was taking. But how could that be? She saw the goddamn ants and the spiders on the wall and crawling across the carpet.

But she never once felt the presence of Susie. And perhaps then she *was not* part of whatever the integral equation was. I thought (angrily): Ask the goddamn kids will you because they are having weird dreams, I'm having weird dreams and you are just about as hunky dory as can be!

Even stranger things started to happen.

The few times I played the CD of Ravel's Bolero, there was no music on the disc, just soft, evil laughter. I threw it in the trash.

I would wake up and find myself wandering about the house and I would find the television on and the electric oven full on in the kitchen or the taps turned on and one night, I woke and found myself wandering around the garden with a knife in my hand and it was then I began to wonder if it *had* actually been me who had killed the dog and not Susie. Perhaps she had influenced me and I had actually done it! But then I reminded myself that no fingerprints were found on the knife. I couldn't explain that. There appeared to be no rational explanation for anything that was happening.

How could I tell Anna about this, that it might actually have been me who killed the dog and I had done it because the evil spirit of a past lover had told me to do it? Do you know what? Had I told her this, I would have found myself very securely locked away and told I was experiencing another breakdown – or that I was totally and utterly insane!

But then a few more weird things happened over the next week or so. A few nights later and this time, I knew – I just knew – it was Susie, I fell asleep in a chair in the lounge and didn't wake until around three in the morning. I dragged myself upstairs and as I was passing Joseph's room, I heard him moving about. I went in and found him sitting in his sofa chair.

"What's wrong, Joe?" I asked him.

"Nothing."

"Seems like a pretty big nothing to me. It's three in the morning, your eyes are all red, as if you have been crying. Have you been crying? It's okay to tell me. I want to know what the problem is."

"You wouldn't believe me if I told you."

"Well, if you don't tell me, I'll never find out. And so, we'll be back to square one."

He hesitated for a few moments, then said, "I keep dreaming of this weird lady. I don't know who she is but I keep dreaming about her and she does bad things. In my dream, I saw her kill Doozy. And tonight, she was doing dirty things – with you."

"What do you mean by dirty things?"

"Well, things to do with sex but it wasn't normal. Not like we've been taught in school."

I told him not to worry about it, that it was only a bad dream and it might be best not to talk to anyone about it just yet. Wait to see what happens. I think I managed to convince him that it was the aftershock of losing Doozy.

I came down early one morning a few days later because lying awake, I swore I could hear someone moving around in the lounge. Anna was still sleeping soundly and I could hear no movement from the kids' rooms. But to be on the safe side, I looked into each and they were all sleeping soundly. I went downstairs into the lounge and switched the light on. The water in the fish tank was red with blood and all the goldfish (there were eight of them) were floating on the surface.

I spent an hour cleaning the fish tank because I didn't want the kids to see this first thing in the morning. Hell, I didn't want them to see it at all! And lying there on the bottom of the tank among the grit and sand was the blue tanzanite pendant Susie used to like wearing. This time, I put it in my pocket, went out of the house (at four in the goddamn morning!!) and got into the car. I drove about ten miles before I came to a fast flowing river. I dumped the pendant in the river and hoped that would go some way into getting Susie to leave us alone.

I knew – I just knew one hundred per cent – it was Susie because how else did the tanzanite pendant keep appearing? I had thrown it into the trash can back at my apartment, yet it appeared months later. I threw it into our own trash can, yet it appeared on Amelia's bed the night she had her nightmare. That time, I remember putting it in the trash can outside and the trash collection guys would take it away when they called a few days hence. But then it appeared in the bottom of the fish tank.

Something told me I had wasted my time in dumping the pendant in a river miles from home. If it was indeed Susie doing all of this, she would find the damned thing and leave it for me again.

****

I explained to the kids next morning that the fish had died because there had been a fault in the air pump but I told Anna what I had found.

"How can all three children dream about the same weird lady? Glen, is this house haunted or what? I am frightened. Not for me but for the children. This weird stuff never started happening until you returned. What do you know about this Glen? And whose blood was it anyway?"

"I don't know. It certainly wasn't mine."

And then for some reason totally unknown to me (but perhaps it was finally to clear my conscience), I told Anna about Susie and the fact that she ended her life because I rejected her. I didn't tell her about the weird sex but only because I didn't think it was relevant in any way. It wasn't important enough for this discussion. I told her how Susie started getting clingy and how I ended our relationship. More to the point, how Susie ended it by throwing herself off the roof of my apartment building.

"Glen, why haven't you told me about this before?"

"I don't know, Anna," I said to her. "I didn't think she was that important to what is happening. I thought it must be me and my breakdown. I don't know how to answer you. I've told you everything I know and so I can't tell you any more. This is an impossible situation. You see things like this in creepy movies but for God's sake, it cannot, simply cannot, happen in real life. So what else can I tell you? You know about Susie and I don't know what else I can tell you"

"Glen, I trusted you and took you back because you were ill – now I want the complete truth and it has to be the truth because I do not intend to be made a fool of — not a second time."

"I can't tell you any more because there is no more to tell. What do you want me to tell you? Yes, we are being haunted and I'll go get a priest to perform an exorcism?"

"Is this one of your mistresses, Glen? Because if it is, you had better sort this out. The very last thing I need in this house is an Alexandra Forrest bunny boiler. God forbid!"

We talked about it, argued about it but we got nowhere fast and she eventually stormed out of the house and went to work. The feeling of an evil presence in the house became overpowering on that day and I just stayed in my room until Anna returned with the children.

"Glen, you will have to drop the kids off at school tomorrow. I have an early morning meeting and I have to be there. Will you be okay with that?"

"Yes, I'll take them."

But I didn't take them to school. How can you take dead children to school? Well, you can but you would get some pretty weird looks and somebody would call the cops. As it turned out, they came anyway.

****

"School's out for today, kids," I told them. "Mom's had to go to work early and my car won't start. I'll explain to your school." They all attended the same school and for whatever reason, I was grateful for that. I called the school and told the secretary they had the sniffles. It seemed as good an excuse as any.

I left them to do whatever kids do when they have an unexpected day off school. Joseph sat at his computer in his room while Amelia and Charlie played with their dolls and the doll's house in their own room.

I went into my own bedroom, lay on the bed and fell asleep. I was dreaming again and there was Susie with a big kitchen knife in her hand.

"Take it, Glen," she said. "You know what you have

to do with it."

"Don't make me do it, Susie. I'll give you anything you want – just don't make me kill them."

"Did you see how easy it was for me to make you kill the dog – knife across its throat and then the knife in its side? Nothing to it."

"Susie, no. I'll give you anything you want."

"What can you give me that I want? I'm simply an ethereal existence – in the atmosphere or in your mind. It doesn't matter. So again, what is it you can give me? There is nothing in the spirit world I want and things in the material world are no longer any use to me – I just want you and only you. There must be no one else in our lives. Use what you have, Glen – use it on them. I don't want them around. It has to be just you and me. Do it, Glen. Do it! Do it! DO IT!"

I just wanted to wake from this terrifying nightmare and for everything to be okay with Anna and me. But Susie was too strong for me. All this time she had been haunting the house, haunting me, she had been working on me, making me weaker and weaker, bending me to her will.

She bit me again and it was like she was sucking the life force out of me. I tried to ward her off but I was too weak and she was too strong. She was always too strong. She was strong in life and now in death, she was a monster vampire bitch and I was sinking fast beneath her magnetic pull.

And then I was wandering in a blood-coloured mist and I remember the knife going into Joseph's neck, throat, chest and stomach and then it seemed I was floating through the house. I was lost until I found my way to the girls' bedroom and all of their dolls had turned to devil dolls with evil grins on their faces and a look of total insanity in their glass eyes and teeth gnashing and gnashing, ready to bite. The doll's house looked old and haunted, like Mockingbird

Heights. Jesus Christ, it was Mockingbird Heights!

Amelia was screaming –"No daddy! No daddy!"– and Charlie was just sitting there whimpering and in deep shock and saying, "Nasty dollies, daddy. Nasty dollies house," and the next thing I remember was a river of blood and it was all sticky and red and somewhere in the background – I don't know where it was coming from – Susie was screaming, "KILLED YOUR KIDS! KILLED YOUR KIDS! KILLED YOUR KIDS!" but it was a far distant sound and it frightened me because I didn't know where I was or indeed when I was.

I went back to sleep and I had peaceful dreams because all of a sudden, Susie was gone.

****

I was woken by Anna screaming. All I could hear was Anna screaming and screaming, so loud that it must have fetched Jack from next door. I think it was him who called the cops. Two cops had got hold of me and they put cuffs on me. I remember them taking a carving knife off me and the knife was covered in blood.

There was a doctor with a stethoscope examining me and everything seemed so confused and I wondered what the hell was going on with all of these people in the house; cops, doctors, paramedics. And Maisie from next door was trying to comfort Anna.

"She made me do it," I said to the cops but they were not listening. "It was Susie. She made me do it. Susie! Goddamn you!"

One of the cops said, "Why did you kill your kids and then go back later to do what you did to them?"

The cop told me what I had apparently done to the kids after stabbing them to death but, cut me some slack here – you really do not want to know the finer details. They are not pleasant by any stretch of the imagination and no wonder Anna was screeching her head off. The doctor gave her a sedative but it didn't seem to be working and the cops wouldn't let me comfort my wife. They thought Maisie was doing a better job.

Of course, I couldn't answer the cops when they asked me these questions. And that was a major problem – I had no answers for anything. I had no answers for anyone. At least nothing rational.

Somebody helped me wash myself down and change my clothes (I was covered in blood and gore and God alone knows what else and the dirty clothes were kept for evidence – as if they needed any).

I had done what Susie made me do! I had done what she wanted me to do.

Even as they were putting me in the police car, I could hear Anna screaming. It was such a soulful sound and I wondered if she herself would keep her sanity.

But at my sentencing hearing, she screamed in a different way; she screamed hell and damnation at me and what she would do to me if ever she got her hands on me and she had to be restrained and removed from the court (she must have been experiencing a surge of immense strength and resolve because it took four burly court officials to remove her from the room) and her language was the most utterly disgusting and awful language I have ever heard any woman use.

I think the judge sympathised with her.

Perdition: Summer 2017

Sometimes, I think this is all a dream. I keep thinking I will wake up in bed next to Anna and then I'll get up and wash and shave, get dressed and get the kids up. I'll go downstairs to make them breakfast and I'll let Doozy out so he can do whatever dogs do first thing in the morning and then he'll come back inside, have a bowl of food and then go next door to Jack and Maisie's to stay for the day because we won't leave him in the house alone. And then I'll go off to work and Anna will take the kids to school.

But that is fantasy. It isn't real. It never can be real; not now. What I now exist in is real and what makes it worse is that I know I can't turn back time and make it all unhappen. This is reality and I have woken up to it.

I know you think I'm a, cold-hearted, calculating bastard for doing what I did to my children. But Susie forced me to do it. In death, in the spirit world where she now exists, her influence, her strength, must be a billionfold what it was in life because I couldn't resist or fight against her. I tried. Believe me, I tried but in the end, I lost the war.

I don't know how you can say such bad things about me when inside of myself I cry for the loss of my children. I really do. What I did to them was truly horrifying beyond belief and I remember a few of the female jurors (and a few of the men) at my trial breaking down in tears when the autopsy report was read out.

You see, I'm a very sensitive guy and I will openly weep at the beauty of a Botticelli portrait or a Beethoven Piano Concerto (the first is my favourite and I no longer like Maurice Ravel) and thus, how can I be accused of being so insensitive?

If you are going to blame somebody, blame Susie, that selfish, self-centred and nasty minded evil bitch. She has brought far more pain to me, literally and figuratively, than any human could ever possibly bear. So perhaps I should welcome death just so that I can meet up with her again and tear her to pieces just like she made me do to my children. Because if my strength increases in death, that is precisely what I will do to her. Or is that statement just me showing a little bravado? Is it my anger talking? Yes, I think it is and because of what is waiting for me on the other side of life, I am afraid of death.

****

I sit in this room all on my own. There is only one door and that is always kept locked. Keeping the door locked prevents the laughing mad lady on the other side getting in to hurt me. I don't know what her name is but I don't think it's Susie. Yes, even in here she haunts me; day and night she haunts me and I don't know how she gets into this cell because the door is always locked.

Perhaps there is another laughing mad lady on the other side of the door and it is she who cannot get into this cell. I wonder why that is? But I guess I have to tolerate this until the day I die. That is a day I am not looking forward to because I know who and what is waiting for me on the other side. Susie is waiting for me, with open arms and her cane or whip or whatever she uses in Hell. And my children are waiting for me too. And you must know how vicious children can be. These three don't like their daddy any more; I know that much and I don't have to be sane to know it.

I can hear her, in the dead of night, in the dimly lit corridor on the other side of the steel door and it is Susie after all. This I have decided upon. It is Susie and she does it just to torment me. She doesn't want to talk to me or make fun of me or rip the skin off my back with a whip or cane. She just wants to sit outside my cell door in the early hours of the morning and laugh that low creepy laugh of hers. I curl up in the opposite corner and try to hide because I am very frightened she will get in and hurt me.

****

Then one night, several years into my sentence, I woke in the early hours of the morning because someone was calling to me. The sound was a distant sound when I was awake (but it was louder when I was dreaming – but was I dreaming? I don't know. It seemed like I was) but it gradually became clearer.

"Who is there? Who are you?" I said to the darkness.

"Who did you think it was Glen?" a young child's voice said.

"Susie?"

"No, not Susie. Why did you think it was Susie?"

"I don't know. Sometimes, she and talks to me but not for a while now. And maybe she isn't the mad bad lady outside my cell who keeps laughing in the early hours."

"No, Glen, I'm not Susie. I'm – I haven't got a name but you can give me a name, can't you?"

"Okay, I think I shall call you Donna. How would that be?"

"Donna. I like that."

"So who are you?" I asked.

"I am Athenia's aborted child. That no account bastard Ethan Saul raped my mother and Pandora, her mother, made her get rid of me. Can you dig that, Glen? It's complicated I know. But she asked me to carry on where she left off."

And then there was a swishing sound and then pain across my back.

"In the realm of evil spirits, anything is possible," Donna said. "It was Susie at first when she killed herself and forced you to kill your dog and your children. Hey, I missed that. I bet that was good. But she has tired of you. She has gone a' haunting elsewhere – poor bastard whoever he is.

"Think I'll park myself outside your door a while. No, no, I won't do that because I don't want to vie with your kids – they were first in line and I don't want to jump ahead. Now you know it was them all the time. But I'll be back sometime. My niece has loaned me a few – implements? Until next time, Glen.

"Oh and by the way, if your wife dies before you, she will most likely take her place with the kids scratching at your door. Looks like she might make it too, the way she keeps swilling back the vodka like there was no tomorrow. Catch you later."

******

I remember a conversation I once had with Dietrich Weissman (in one of my more lucid periods) and he said, "I would rather take a more practical approach, not only because my profession requires it but because mental instability always involves the mind, the self."

"Are you suggesting that I'm to blame for my illness?"

"Yes and no. The illness comes from within you. There are no ghosts, no evil spirits. I am not saying you have deliberately manufactured this entity of a previous lover but rather, I firmly believe it is the guilt of that affair and then suddenly ending it – and the shocking way it did in fact end - which is playing tricks on your mind.

"Stress – and I honestly believe that stress is playing a very important role in your illness – can do strange things to us."

"But she made me kill my children!"

"No, Glen. Nobody made you do anything of the kind. You suffered a major nervous breakdown and the fact that you murdered your children, killed your dog, well, I hate to sound so clinical, but those events were simply symptoms of your disturbed mind."

"Why bother with this now? I'm in here for the rest of my life so why are you bothering?"

"I have to have some closure on your case. It's that simple. And there have to be notes for future personnel who take the case over from me."

"Are you planning to go away?"

"No, not quite yet. I have been offered a post at Johns Hopkins and I'm seriously considering it."

"Susie isn't haunting me any more."

"Since when?"

"Oh for quite some time. A couple of months, I think. I don't know. It's easy for me to lose track of time. Time has no meaning for me in here, in this cell. I sit in this cell and it is all there is. I wish there was something different."

"Well, totally dependent on your behaviour, I can possibly arrange periods of exercise for you outside of your cell. But you keep slipping back into your unreal world and that is what I have to tackle first and foremost.

"But you still talk in that strange woman's voice you have."

"I keep telling you – how many times must I tell you? – that it is – was – Susie and not me. This time, it's Donna."

"Who is Donna? I never read anything about Donna in anything you have written."

"She is Athenia's aborted child – or at least her evil spirit."

He sighed a desperate sigh (I was only trying to help him along) and said, "Okay, Glen, I think that will be enough for one day. When you want to talk to me again, let me know through the usual channels."

He walked out of my cell and it was several months before we spoke again. And that happened to be the last time I spoke to him because then he moved to his new post at Johns Hopkins. I think he still has an interest in my case though. But the exercise periods never happened.

****

They only allow me a laptop computer. No pens or pencils in case I try to poke out my eyes or stab myself or even attack the orderlies.

Why would I wish to commit suicide when I know who is waiting for me on the other side? Perhaps if I live for many, many years, Susie (or Donna) will have gone by the time I kick my bucket. But somehow, I don't believe that. The both of them can wait for an eternity and they will have what they want.

My children can also wait for the same length of time and so can Anna if she dies before I do.

Sometimes, I think this is all a dream and I will wake up and everything will be as it was before Anna threw me out of the house that time of my affair with the *au pair*. If only I hadn't slept with her that day, maybe none of this would have happened. Too many ifs and buts to work on here. Think I'll leave the analysis alone for a while. But looking at things realistically, no, it isn't a dream. This is reality. This is the front gate main entrance to Perdition and it frightens me.

Well, that's it. You know all of the important facts,

but I've taken a little poetic licence where I didn't know what was said (couldn't really have known) and put my own words in. But the main facts, all of them, are there. Believe what you want; I don't care.

But there are a number of questions I think you might be asking (and I asked them myself a number of times before the answers came to me in a moment of inspiration): why did Anna not dream of the 'funny lady' as the kids described her? Why did Anna not suffer Susie's physical or mental abuse as I did? Why did Susie leave Anna completely out of the equation? Why did she not make me slash and hack Anna to death as well as the kids?

Answer – because there had to be someone left alive to really hate me. There had to be someone left alive for me to be afraid of and believe me, I am shit scared of Anna breaking into the asylum and getting to me. You think that is an impossibility? Not to me, it isn't.

But it was Susie's way of dealing with Anna. After all, why should Susie be the only loser? Why should Anna have a comfortable life, a nice home, three kids and a husband? Susie didn't want me to be happy and neither did she want Anna to be happy and things finally worked out the way Susie wanted it.

Oh boy but she had this worked out to an infinitesimal degree of absolute perfection. Didn't I say a while back that Susie never made plans that went wrong? Okay, so her plan concerning me veered off the path somewhere but eventually, she found her way back. She had a Plan B on hold just in case Plan A went a smidge haywire – as Plan A's sometimes do. After all, how can you accurately plan for the human condition and not have something go even just a teensy bit wrong?

But perhaps the most important question of all and if you don't believe a word I have written, there is really no point in asking this question. But I'll ask it anyway – but on your behalf.

Do ghosts and evil spirits truly exist?

You bet your sweet bippy they do!

Report DW/GJM/0332/11-12-17:
Dietrich Weissman: Fall 2017

This work is an unofficial statement written by Glen Joseph McKinley, sentenced to a term of life imprisonment for murdering his three children. Throughout his trial and ever since, he has been incarcerated in the Brooklyn-Queens Institute for the Criminally Insane.

The statement is unofficial because it is not to be accepted as a sworn statement of fact since its author is deemed to be mentally and rationally incapable of making such a statement, even though at times he appears to be a rationally thinking person.

However, at times, he screams until he can scream no more and thus, he has to be sedated and secured in a strait jacket. Then for days, weeks, he is silent and stares into empty space. Yet at other times, he is quite rational, intelligent, talkative, reasonable. I understand him as much as any psychiatrist can understand his patient but there are certain aspects of his case which, as yet, are beyond my own understanding. Such as:

1 Sometimes, weal marks appear on his back or a redness or what look like stripes made with a bamboo cane may appear on his buttocks. I cannot explain why or how this happens. It reminds me of a stigmata and stigmata is the only rational explanation I have for this phenomenon. I have no other intelligence as to its origin.

2 Sometimes, he appears to be talking to someone who is not there but he does not like to be disturbed when these conversations are going on.

3 Sometimes, he has a real terror of something only he can see or hear. It is like the 'person' he talks to but only he can see her. Susie is her name and he says she is the evil spirit of his lover who committed suicide by leaping from

the roof of his apartment building.

4 Sometimes – and this is why I doubt the existence of a so-called evil spirit – he talks in a high-pitched voice, a woman's voice, and he says this is Susie (who is actually talking to him and through him). And then he will revert back to his own voice when he is talking back to her. These conversations can last for hours. If indeed it is Glen who is mimicking a feminine voice, he is very, very good at it.

5 But the woman's voice has now changed. It is the voice of a female child, a very high-pitched voice, as you would expect from a child. He says this is the spirit of Athenia de Francia's aborted child, such child being the result of her being raped by her own father and the unborn foetus was aborted at two months development. When he says the child speaks to him, does he mean a small child of, say, five or six years of age (which is what the voice actually sounds like) or does he really believe he is talking to a two month old aborted foetus?

6 He says that it was Susie who drove him to murder his three children. She also, apparently, drove him to kill the family pet, a Dalmatian dog. Again, it is difficult to discover the truth of this. I can of course put forward conjecture but conjecture does not necessarily uncover the truth and therefore does not resolve the issue. This case is full of conjecture and it all has to be unravelled at some time.

In his periods of rationality, he has written his 'statement' on a laptop computer (loaned to him during such periods of rationality: strangely, he tells us when to take it away, as if he has foreknowledge of when he is going to become violent or when he is going to be inactive for weeks or months, at which point, he will have no use for it). But it is not likely to help his case because he is quite insane. Perhaps though, hopefully, it will satisfy his own inner tensions and help to relax him. And thus, he continues to write on the laptop. And strangely, it all makes sense – of a sort. I mean, none of it can be described as being the ramblings of a madman.

He completed the work several months ago and then slipped into a catatonic trance. He came out of it a few weeks ago and he is talking again – to the child (foetus?). Apparently, Donna is her name and it is a name which he suggested to her when she first metamorphosed or became a 'part' of him and his illness. He is again holding what he would describe as a 'normal' conversation by talking in a woman's (female child's) voice. At least Glen thinks she is real. Who knows?

Sometimes, the two entities chat together with him. This is really the most remarkable case of multi-personality disorder I have ever experienced.

I continue to investigate his case and it may be many years before it is finally unravelled. My personal feelings are that I do not believe the case will ever be resolved, even beyond his death.

I have given a number of my most senior students prolific notes on this case and it will be interesting to see what they come up with regarding either a final solution or further treatment.

Dietrich Weissman,

Emeritus Professor of Forensic Psychiatry,

Johns Hopkins University School of Medicine,

November 12 2017.

Printed in Great Britain
by Amazon